A SUMMER AT THE NIAGARA OF THE SOUTH

ROMANCE AT THE GILDED AGE RESORTS
BOOK EIGHT

DENISE WEIMER

Cover design by: Carpe Librum Book Design

ISBN-13: 978-1-942265-97-9

PROLOGUE

*P*eople can pass it by without even realizing it. Every autumn, droves of leaf-lookers bound for the highlands of Georgia do just that. Well, it's not surprising when there're but a few buildings left, no passenger trains belching black smoke into the bright jewel sky, and the mighty river that was once a roar in the gorge is now just a murmur by the road throughout most of the year. The dam harnessed the power of Tallulah Falls but opened the sieve of the town's lifeblood. Then the fires devoured almost all evidence of the grand hotels and homes. It's been mostly quiet here since. The tourists have forgotten "The Niagara of the South."

But I can't forget. I have only a few faded photos of ladies in tall hats and bustled skirts, on the arms of gentlemen who look somber in their black coats, yet I can close my eyes and hear the music and laughter of a bygone era. I think often, and the folks in these parts still sometimes talk, about a red-haired beauty who could sing like an angel—how she lighted here with a broken voice, and a broken heart, and what happened to her, my great-great-grandma...

CHAPTER 1

North Georgia, late June, 1886

*B*y the time the train pulled out of Cornelia, the dusky haze of an early summer's evening embraced the darkening horizon. A red sun hung about an hour's worth above, promising light and heat for the final leg of their journey north, but not much more.

The stocky, middle-aged man who had just boarded took a seat near them. He adjusted his wire-rimmed spectacles, trying to be inconspicuous in his study.

Grace Galveston turned her face toward the window. Even in areas where people would not readily recognize her, her vibrant red-gold hair drew stares. She didn't have it in her now to be sociable. The travel that day from Athens had been tiring. And the pall from Savannah, like a dark cloud, still hung heavy over her.

Aunt Martha shifted on the seat beside her. The guidebook nestled in the folds of her skirt slid to the floor.

Immediately, the man bent to retrieve it, saying, "Permit me." With a smile and a flourish, he handed it back.

Aunt Martha thanked him, studying him with her sharp eye.

"You are, madam, traveling to Tallulah?"

"We are," she admitted.

"There is much your guidebook will not tell you."

"I am sure." Martha Hampton raised one eyebrow and seemed to consider whether this interloper was worthy of further address.

Obviously not about to lose the opportunity to meet this dignified-looking woman with her silver-streaked brown hair and tailored traveling costume, the man hastened to make his introduction. He was Professor Willard Schmidt of the Sibley Institute in nearby Mt. Airy. His green eyes glowed with pleasure as Grace turned to acknowledge him, but to her vast relief, his attentions fastened not on her, as she was accustomed to, but on Aunt Martha, his peer in age.

This enabled Grace to listen to their conversation while keeping an eye on the lush hills rolling past. It was not hard to imagine them still populated only with Cherokee Indians and a few rugged settlers, as they had been at the beginning of the century, before the Trail of

Tears and the "discovery" of Tallulah by the outside world.

"Is Mt. Airy a large town?" inquired Aunt Martha.

"Not by the standards of New York, to be sure." Professor Schmidt offered a sheepish smile. Aunt Martha had just told him the city from which they hailed. "But it is widely known as a resort town due to its healthy air. There is a sizeable Swiss colony, more than one school, mercantiles, orchards...and Colonel Wilcox just completed a most impressive hotel."

"Ah, to rival those in Tallulah." Martha raised her brows.

"Well, even our mountain air pales in comparison to the gorge and its many waterfalls." The professor chuckled. "I find myself returning again and again. I am lucky to have friends in the town. I'm sure you've read that the gorge is over a thousand feet deep, and in less than a mile, the river descends five hundred feet."

"Yes, in a series of about six falls. I look forward to seeing it." Aunt Martha's firm lips relaxed into a smile.

"You will not be disappointed. Hopefully, you will feel justified in coming all this way, to our Niagara instead of yours." The gentleman waited, clearly in hopes of an explanation of their motives for the trip. When none were forthcoming, he proved his breeding by not pressing further. But he did ask, "How was it that you came to hear of Tallulah Falls? Through some book on travel or health resorts, perhaps?"

Aunt Martha hesitated. "I did read up on the destination before we embarked, but my knowledge of its existence goes back to my childhood near Savannah."

"I see." Professor Schmidt assessed her intently, but her rigid back again discouraged his curiosity. "Yes, planters from the coast built some lovely homes in Clarkesville. And students from The University of Georgia made the trek to the falls long before there was a railroad. Tallulah has had rail service only four years now, but my! What a difference it has already made. Grand hotels with bands playing every night during the summer, all the popular amusements, droves of tourists..."

And he was a veritable tourist guide. Grace flattened her mouth. Despite his informative qualities, their gregarious companion began to annoy her. Welcome silence reigned for a few minutes as Grace fingered a ruffle on her royal-blue skirt and gazed out the window.

Mountain views were indeed soothing. She hadn't exactly expected to be soothed in Savannah, but she had hoped to find something she was looking for. Some sense of identity, of belonging.

Aunt Martha had not wanted to go. She preferred to remember things as they had been. But Grace insisted on the stop, and even Aunt Martha knew she had no right to deny her niece a glimpse of what might have been her birthright. Their stay in the charming environs of Savannah lasted only a short time, though. Her aunt was unwilling to risk a chance encounter and possible snubbing from any previous acquaintances.

Grace's heart had stirred as they arrived at what had been Hampton Hall. But an aching loneliness swept her as she walked the grounds and gazed a long time at the ruins—the brick chimneys that jutted up as a reminder of past grandeur, one fallen, blackened column a reminder of loss. She tried to envision her mother on the veranda welcoming suitors as Maum Sally had often described, or playing hide-and-seek with Aunt Martha in the orchard.

She'd listened for the echo of imagined laughter and the whisper of hoopskirts until she knew exactly what Maum Sally would have told her had she still been alive and at Grace's side—"Don't you go lookin' for no ghosts, Miss Gracie. Not here. You get on with your own life an' don't spend it pokin' about in the rubble of the past like Miss Martha."

Trouble was, she wasn't feeling too confident about her own life.

"Ladies, we're coming up to the first of several trestles." The voice of the professor broke into Grace's troubled reverie. "This one over Hazel Creek is a triple-decker."

As the engine steamed out over an amazing wooden bridge, Grace's interest piqued. She leaned forward and gazed down at the creek at least fifty feet below.

She gasped. "I see why it took so long for the railroad to reach Tallulah."

"Yes, it was arduous work, putting it in." The professor sat back. "At which hotel will you be staying?"

"The Cliff House," she answered without consideration, still looking out her window.

"I thought as much. The owner, Mr. Rufus LaFayette Moss, is quite the man of the town. He is one of our commissioners and quite involved with the railroad. He's raised his family in Athens. Mr. Moss and his wife Elizabeth live at Pine Terrace during the summer months."

"My concern is, does he run a smart hotel?" Aunt Martha lifted her chin.

"Oh, yes, ma'am. The finest. It sits on forty acres and has over ninety rooms. Its dining room seats over two hundred and fifty."

Martha gave something that resembled a sniff. "My guidebook told me that much." She tapped the volume. "The Fifth Avenue Hotel is six stories, with six hundred rooms and an elevator. I doubt anything in Tallulah can outdo that. But I do hope the food and amusements are of acceptable quality."

Uncowed, Professor Schmidt smiled with amazing patience. "Delicious gourmet food, the goods brought in fresh by local farmers. Hiking, lawn tennis, bowling, ping pong, billiards, cards, horse-back and buggy rides. The band in residence is from Athens and renders the finest music for dancing nightly, in exchange for room and board. The hotel is named for The Cliff House Hotel in San Francisco, where the Mosses honeymooned."

"Aunt Martha, I'm sure we will be most comfortable." Grace touched her arm. Really, did her aunt have to be such a snob? "We aren't seeking grand amusements, anyway, just some quiet and relaxation."

The professor cocked his head. "Relaxation you may find, but The Cliff House is centrally located. It's the heart of the social scene."

Grace cut a sharp glance at her aunt. Martha must have known this when she made the reservations. Could her aunt not cease to thrust her into the middle of the activity even while on vacation?

Martha ignored her, maintaining her prim reserve. "I'm just ready to be there. It seems we've been traveling forever." The nervous flutter of her hands betrayed an uncharacteristic fraying around the edges.

Willard Schmidt bowed his head in a humble gesture. "If I can be of service in helping you to your hotel, it would be my pleasure. The Cliff House is right across the tracks from the depot, but I could collect your baggage and escort you to the desk."

Aunt Martha smiled. "We would be in your debt."

Really? Though considered plain, and a lifelong spinster, Aunt Martha had never warmed to the few men who had noticed her in recent years. Perhaps the gallant attentions of this Georgia resident appealed to her aunt, somehow seeping past the hardened exterior bred by circumstances and life in a northern city.

As they neared the town, one final, impressive wooden trestle would have given a spectacular view down into the gorge. Unfortunately, the quickly descending darkness made only a black yawning chasm of the scene.

"You can look forward to the wonder of starting tomorrow by viewing Tempesta Falls from The Cliff House's five-story observation tower," Professor Schmidt told her with a twinkle in his eyes. The intuitive man had noted her disappointment.

Adequate light remained to appreciate the beauty of an ornate, two-story building riding the swell of land just to their left. Lights gleamed beyond the intricate porches, and a cupola crowned the roof. Grace caught a glimpse of a splashing fountain. The professor informed them that this was The Grand View Hotel.

"Why did you not put us there, Aunt Martha?" Grace asked.

The older lady merely lifted a shoulder, reminding Grace that it was not her duty to explain. But she said, "The Cliff House has a well-established reputation."

Professor Schmidt had the good manners not to remind the lady of her earlier uncertainties on that score. "This is The Grand View's first year in business. Mr. Young will see to it that his hotel is the equal of Mr. Moss's. In fact, you probably would have found The Grand View at capacity, anyway, since Mr. Young engaged Professor Leon to come this next month."

Whoever that was. Probably some botanist conducting a boring lecture. Grace was too tired to care.

Lights winked welcome from the town's buildings clustered on the south rim of the gorge. The train slowed to a crawl, loudly clanging its bell to herald their late arrival. A bustle of activity exploded on the street as they pulled up to a quaint, two-story wooden depot, painted red with white trim along the windows and corner boards.

"Tallulah Falls!" called the conductor. "End of the line!"

As she stood, Grace peered out the window one more time at what must be their hotel. Two-story porches connected two large white structures, looking to be three-and-a-half stories tall. Under a striped awning, a brass band began to play. The cheerful music made her feel like a visiting dignitary as she stepped off the train.

"Our maid is on the second class car," Aunt Martha told Professor Schmidt.

"One moment, and I will return." He raised his finger, then hurried down the platform.

Uniformed porters scurried around, loading luggage in wagons marked *The Robinson House* and *The Grand View*. A turntable would rotate the train to face southward for the return trip to Clarkesville and Cornelia in the morning.

Professor Schmidt returned as promised, carrying two valises. Their pink-cheeked Irish maid, Maureen, followed right behind. A hotel employee had been dispatched with a cart to fetch their larger trunks.

"Ladies, we may proceed to the hotel," said Professor Schmidt.

Before following, Grace breathed deeply. The mountain air, cool with the damp tang of nighttime, danced right to the bottom of her lungs, igniting a tingle of promise. Maybe they had been right to come here.

~

$\mathcal{T}$he next morning, the roar of water drew Grace from sleep like a strong current, tugging her eyelids open. She lay in her four-poster bed in her hotel room fronting the grounds.

"I will take the street-side room," Aunt Martha had said in a tone of noble sacrifice the night before. "We did come here expressly for *you* to rest." Implying they would have hobnobbed at the summer homes of wealthy New Yorkers in Newport otherwise, as Martha had wished.

Her aunt must still be abed. No sound issued from her chamber that joined Grace's by way of Maureen's small sleeping quarters. Only a few muted, distant movements of early risers and the chirping of birds right outside the window could be heard above the thunder of the river. Indeed, the train commotion and the band music had filled her ears until late yesterday. The initial boisterous tunes had waned into soothing strains as she laid her head on her pillow.

She stretched and sat up, catching sight of her reflection in the vanity mirror. Her waist-length hair, the color of russet autumn leaves, framed her dark-brown eyes and milky oval face and fell over the front of her embroidered white cotton nightgown in a riot of thick waves. Too tired last night to allow Maureen to braid it, Grace now grimaced. The poor maid would pay the price for Grace's laziness.

"You the spittin' image of your ma," Maum Sally had always said, "'Cept a bit prettier." A smirk had always accompanied such announcements, as if Sally revealed a secret she was only free to share with Louisa Hampton Galveston long in her grave.

Dear Maum Sally. How Grace would welcome her mothering right now, at this juncture when she felt lost and vulnerable. Well, she would have to settle for the cheerful, if empty-headed, bustle of Maureen, the immigrant her father hired for them when Maum Sally died.

Grace climbed out of bed. After washing up and changing into her undergarments, she knocked softly at Maureen's door.

The young woman's ginger-colored head quickly appeared. "Yes'm?"

"I'm ready to dress."

The servant already wore her typical gray frock. She was certainly not lazy. "Yes, indeed, ma'am." Maureen hastened to Grace's wardrobe and threw open the door. Inside hung the row of colorful dresses the servant had unpacked with haste the night before. "And what will it be, a nice promenade dress?"

"I think the violet one."

The costume Maureen laid across the bed represented the height of New York fashion. The violet of the bodice, with its square neck, pointed waist, and *basque*, or tail, behind, contrasted with lavender and aquamarine in the front plastron and the elaborate drapery of the skirt. Opening a hat box, the young servant unwrapped a tall hat with a trailing veil to match.

"A very exciting morning, is it not?" Maureen fairly oozed enthusiasm. "Imagine, we're in the wilds of *Georgia*."

As though it was the Wild West.

As Maureen adjusted the laces of Grace's corset, designed to produce the perfect *S*-shaped silhouette, Grace pondered all that had brought her here. Really, it had been her role as the Messenger of Peace in Wagner's *Rienzi* that disrupted the flow of her life. Yes, that was decidedly what marked the change. After that, she could no longer float along in the anonymity of her life with Aunt Martha and her voice lessons with Monsieur LeMonte. Important people in the world of opera had taken notice of her. Suddenly, her name was on everyone's lips. Critics predicted a major role for her in The Metropolitan Opera's 1886-87 season...the season yet to be. And Aunt Martha was determined enough for it to happen to take her far from the scene of her ambition, and Grace's stress, all the way to the mountains of North Georgia.

Grace struggled into the tight, three-quarter-length

sleeves of her bodice and allowed Maureen to work the hooks in back. Then, with an apology for the tangles in her hair, she sat at the vanity for Maureen to create a coiffure. She only half listened to the maid's chatter, murmuring a polite "mmm" and "yes" at the proper moments. While Maureen's focus on the frivolous failed to interest her, the girl's professional ministrations, like the clothing, represented a luxury bought by her father's money. Things Grace should always be grateful for.

But she didn't have to think about that right now. She drew a parasol from the wardrobe. "Please ask my aunt to join me at the gorge overlook when she is ready. I'll wait there for her so we can breakfast together."

"Yes'm." Maureen bobbed a curtsy.

As Grace opened the door, wonderful aromas from the kitchen greeted her. She ignored the rumbling reminder from her stomach that she had forgone even her normal morning coffee.

Outside, the grounds of The Cliff House resembled a Monet painting, ladies strolling on the arms of gentlemen in the soft golden light. Grace admired neatly trimmed shrubs, towering trees, and colorful flowerbeds as she took the path to the boardwalks tracing the gorge's rim. A bright flash of red caught her eye. She smiled as a pileated woodpecker began a persistent tattoo high up on a nearby tree.

As she joined a few others on the boardwalk, a roaring deluge nearby took Grace's breath away. She wandered close enough to read the sign that described Tempesta Falls as descending seventy-six feet but not close enough to get soaked by the spray. A catwalk hugging the cliffs led on to the waterfall-side observation tower Professor Schmidt had described the night before. Not much less than a thousand feet below, the river ran its course, hemmed in by rugged granite cliffs and slopes of hardy oaks and pines. The amazing turquoise color of the water made the scene resemble a lost paradise.

She gazed a long time at the rush of water between the two pools far below. It truly was beautiful, wild and free in a way that Niagara wasn't, like the red-tailed hawk that launched from some hidden nest on the far rim and soared above the chasm. She liked the sense of power in the wilderness, the reminder of the artifice of modern society. Finding an isolated bench, she sat, closing her eyes, feeling the gentle breeze. She breathed deeply as minutes ticked by unnoticed. Ah, the solitude.

"Surely, those people don't intend to *bathe* in that pool!"

The strident voice interrupted Grace's daydreams. She looked up to see her aunt, her opera glasses trained on the scene below. She wore a navy walking dress in a style similar to Grace's, including the draped and bustled skirt. Gone were the elegant, dome-like layers of the seventies. The new rage featured a shelf-like protrusion to the rear that elicited many jokes about horses and tea trays. But no matter how ridiculous Martha Hampton might have admitted the style was, she would be the last to make waves in the New York City society she so dearly wanted to conquer.

Grace straightened. "I have heard that people enjoy swimming in some parts of the river."

"But not that part." Martha unfolded a map and jabbed a finger at a section labeled *Hawthorne's Pool.*

"Yes, that's it, just above the falls."

Grace peered down at the figures near the mysterious jewel-like pool. Steep, rugged cliffs on the north rim sheltered the spot. "It does look tranquil and inviting."

"The same mistake Reverend Hawthorne made in 1837."

"You knew this Reverend Hawthorne?" Grace raised an eyebrow.

"No, no, according to my guidebook," Martha replied impatiently. Grace suppressed a chuckle at her aunt's tendency to gather all the knowledge, and therefore all the control, possible in any situation. "He was from Athens. He preached on a Sunday morning in Clarkesville and then came here with a group of friends. They decided to find a spot to camp. Reverend Hawthorne stayed behind for a swim. Some say, all they ever found were his clothes and pocket watch, placed on a pine sapling."

"And does his ghost haunt the gorge?" Grace couldn't resist asking with mock-wide eyes.

Martha smacked at her with her fan, not even cracking a smile. "There you go being pert again."

"Heaven forbid."

"Grace, if you're going to progress during this visit, you really should let go of a bit of that cynicism. No wonder you can't sing with all that bottled up inside."

Grace withdrew into herself, for her aunt's words hit closer to the truth than she wanted to admit. "Perhaps you mistake the intent of my joking. There's nothing wrong with simply having a bit of fun."

"Fun," said Martha, "is laughing, being with other people, dancing, doing things, not going off by one's self or making glib remarks."

Grace sighed. She did not point out that even though Martha frequently sought out company, she did not often laugh, and she certainly never danced.

"But for now, let's begin with breakfast. A good hearty meal, and then you'll feel up to a hike." Aunt Martha faced the hotel like a general going to battle.

"A hike?" Grace rose uncertainly.

"Yes, there is much to see. Exercise will put the wind back in your sails. I understand that there is an even larger falls just below this one."

"But surely...you...?" The picture of her aunt forging through the wilderness failed to materialize in Grace's mind.

"Of course not. I'm too old for such strutting about. I'll find a nice companion for you, and I'll see about getting some postcards to send to the right people back home. It wouldn't do for everyone to think we've fallen off the face of the earth."

Of course not.

With Grace following, Martha headed back toward the hotel, never having even commented on the view. "It's too bad Blake Greene isn't here to squire you about..." she muttered under her breath.

Blake was the last person Grace would have chosen as a companion right now. Handsome, tall, and intelligent, the Kentucky-born lawyer was both Southern enough and firmly transplanted to New York City enough to win Martha's approval. The money didn't hurt either. His family raised race-winning thoroughbreds on their farm in the Bluegrass, but Blake had chosen to attend school in New York, thus following in his uncle's footsteps and joining his successful firm. His leisurely courtship of Grace had intensified recently, following the *Rienzi* role that had thrust her into the limelight and the notice of other young bachelors. Blake's interest represented another point of confusion in her life. She would have to face it soon and examine her feelings toward the young man, but she needed this time apart first.

Could Tallulah restore her in the soul-deep way she craved?

CHAPTER 2

*A*unt Martha deemed their mealtime in the well-appointed dining room of The Cliff House "quite satisfactory," even though it failed to produce the desired companion for Grace. They spent the morning in town, looking through shops. Around eleven, Grace gasped as she spotted a soda fountain. A painted sign above the door proclaimed, *Wylie's Refreshments.*

"Oh, let's go in," she urged.

Someone waved to them from a round table near the glass front of the store.

"Why, it's Professor Schmidt...and two ladies." Now it was Martha who sounded surprised.

As they approached, the smiling man rose. He took Martha's hand and bowed over it. "What a pleasure to see you again so soon, Miss Hampton," he declared with disarming earnestness. "Miss Galveston. I had hoped to introduce you to my friends."

"Oh." Aunt Martha studied the ladies, who had risen as well. One was about Martha's age, the other about Grace's. Both wore simple but flattering outfits, while sincere smiles graced their round faces.

"Mrs. Sarah Wylie, and her daughter, Miss Amelia Wylie."

The young, dark-haired lady turned to point. "And that's my father, Howard Wylie, behind the counter."

A tall man in a white apron waved to them with one hand while operating the soda fountain with the other.

"You would think he would actually use the help he hires." Sarah laughed. "But nothing makes him happier than tending his customers personally."

"Well, it is a pleasure to meet you." Martha assessed Amelia with a speculative expression.

"These are the friends who are kind enough to open their home to me," the professor explained. "And they were most intrigued when I told them of the cultured ladies from New York whom I met on the train. Won't you join us?"

"The strawberry sodas are especially delicious." Amelia's face lit with a hopeful smile.

"Just what I had in mind." Grace smiled back at her.

The professor pulled out and held the lightweight chairs as they settled their bustled skirts and drew up to the table. Then he hastened to the counter with their orders.

"My father was just in Atlanta and tried a new drink at Jacob's Pharmacy. They called it Coca-Cola. He thinks it will soon be the craze. Imagine, if the hit drink of the country came out of the South!" The sparkle in Amelia's blue eyes belied the possible sarcasm of her comment. "Of course, we know New York is the place *everything* is happening. Have you seen The Statue of Liberty? The Washington Monument? Did you get to attend the demonstration of Mr. Bell's telephone?"

Grace laughed and held up a hand. "Yes, sort of, and no." Even though the girl couldn't be but a year or two younger than Grace—and she herself had just turned twenty—there was a refreshing openness, a naiveté, about her. Especially compared to many of New York society and the world of opera, where people often said what they did not mean in their quest to better their social standing.

Grace had read a great deal in the newspapers about the amazing sculpture, "Liberty Enlightening the World," given in friendship to The United States by France, and had even driven to the waterfront to view its construction on Bedloe's Island. "The statue is truly amazing, over three hundred feet tall," she told her attentive little audience. "It is made of copper sheets on a steel framework. Workers have been reassembling the pieces ever since they arrived last summer. President Cleveland will dedicate the statue this fall."

"Oh, how I wish I could be there." Amelia sighed dreamily.

"As to The Washington Monument, I have not been to see it at the National Mall, but we did get to view the pyramid when it was on display in New York, at Tiffany's."

"You know it's the largest piece of aluminum in the world, and extremely costly." Aunt Martha looked up as Professor Schmidt returned with their sodas. Ever the paragon of proper etiquette, she explained to him, "We were just discussing the sites and innovations in New York City."

"I see." His eyes lit with interest.

"Tiffany's..." Amelia murmured. She eyed their jewelry and dresses. "Do you go there often?"

"Goodness, no—"

"But you would love to walk the Ladies Mile and see all the grand mansions being built on Fifth Avenue," Aunt Martha cut in. "The marble chateau Alva and Willie Vanderbilt put up next to St. Thomas is the most breathtaking. There are unicorns and sea serpents and cupids on the roof, with copper cresting."

Sarah and Amelia exchanged subtle glances and sipped their sodas.

Martha laughed lightly, oblivious to their with-drawal. "People still talk about Mrs. Vanderbilt's masquerade ball of eighty-three, the year they christened their new home. Her sister-in-law, Alice, came as an electric light, in a white satin gown trimmed with diamonds and a battery-operated headdress, of all things! Can you imagine? Everyone who was anyone was there. I heard that event alone cost $250,000."

"Aunt Martha—"

"And I suppose it did force the old-money Astors to take notice. You wouldn't believe how exclusive Caroline Astor is, she and her social planner, Ward McAllister, with their list of 'The Four Hundred.'" Martha sniffed in disdain. "Her annual ball is *the* event of the season. Anyway, they get along now. The Vanderbilts are content since they pressured the opera's board to build The Met. Now there is enough room for all of them, old money and new. What do they call it, where they sit, Grace?"

"Um...the Diamond Horseshoe." Her face hot, Grace ducked her chin. Martha simply could not believe that everyone would not aspire to such pinnacles of worldly success, and indeed, might find that kind of grandeur excessive or intimidating.

"I must say the Vanderbilts are loyal supporters of the opera, though. I thought Mrs. Vanderbilt's compliments on your performance in *Rienzi* were very gracious." Aunt Martha cast a benevolent glance upon Grace.

"You're an opera singer?" asked both the Wylie ladies, almost in unison.

"Well...yes."

"Why did you not tell us?" Sarah turned on Professor Schmidt.

"I—must admit—I did not know," he said, raising his hands.

"Are you a star?" Amelia's voice was faint with wonder.

Grace shrugged. "I would hardly say so. Lilli Lehmann is the undisputed darling of The Metropolitan Opera."

Amelia sucked in a breath. "Yes, I have heard of her."

"Grace is far too modest." Martha waved her hand. "She will soon have all the acclaim of Ms. Lehmann and more. People are saying she will receive her first major role this fall. That is, if she can rest up enough this summer to return in full strength of voice."

"Oh, my," murmured Sarah Wylie.

Her shoulders tightening, Grace sipped her soda. Her aunt's conversation brought unpleasant memories of the last few months to the fore.

"So are you here to allow the natural wonders of Tallulah to soothe your spirits?" Professor Schmidt favored Grace with a gentle smile.

What a sensitive man. She nodded. "Very aptly spoken."

Martha leaned forward. "Being thrust into the lime-light so suddenly, among other things, has caused stress on Grace's voice. It is such a delicate instrument, you know. Her doctor and instructor both advised strict rest —a complete change of scenery."

"Oh, well, you've come to the perfect place," said

Sarah. "We certainly have the best air and scenery, even mineral springs."

"We enjoyed the view from our hotel grounds down into the gorge this morning. I was telling Grace what a shame it is that I am not robust enough to make the hike to the water's edge." Aunt Martha released an emphatic sigh. "Such exercise would surely do her good."

Sarah opened her eyes wide and turned them upon her daughter, saying with emphasis, "I am sure Amelia would enjoy showing Miss Galveston her favorite trails."

Amelia hesitated, her enthusiasm now subdued. "I —yes—I would be happy to."

Oh dear. Aunt Martha had intimidated her, just as Grace had feared. "You surely already had plans for the day. I don't want to interfere." Amelia at least deserved a means of escape, though maybe, just maybe she wouldn't take it.

"No, no...it's perfectly fine. I usually just loll about here at Father's store on Saturdays. Going with you would be much more interesting. Where would you like to go?"

Grace shrugged, stuffing back the bright smile that attempted to break forth. "You are the local expert. Wherever you suggest."

Amelia told her Hurricane Falls ranked the largest at ninety-six feet, but the clouds of spray enveloping the area made the narrow footpaths treacherous. An alternative number of smaller falls, rapids, or pools offered lovely but tranquil scenery. Sarah countered by insisting Hurricane Falls offered the grandest introduction to Tallulah.

"But you'd definitely have to change." Amelia glanced at Grace. "And wear your sturdiest boots."

Was Amelia trying to test her metal? It didn't seem possible that the sweet young woman would do so out of spite, or to embarrass her. As Grace weighed her motivations, Amelia's face softened, almost as if she were reading Grace's mind. She added, "We can go very slowly."

Professor Schmidt said, "I think she's hoping to make enough of an impression without scaring you off so that you'll stay with us a long time. There's a shortage of young people outside of the tourist season, you know."

"Except for Alice Hargrove," Amelia agreed with a wrinkled nose.

Grace knew all too well about the lack of friends one's own age. Back home, Martha carefully screened all of Grace's potential companions by their social standing. Grace usually found those who met her aunt's requirements to be wanting for sincerity. She assured Amelia she was up to the challenge.

They agreed to meet at an hour after lunch on the porch of Grace's hotel. Just as eager to get out from under Aunt Martha's wing as Martha was to have her go, Grace arrived early. She gratefully accepted the carved walking stick that Amelia had brought for her use and followed the girl to a trail that descended toward Hurricane Falls. Amelia suggested Grace would enjoy taking The Cliff House catwalks to the observation tower another day.

"A lot of famous people have come here," she said as they brushed past mountain laurel and stepped over tree roots. "Writers, politicians, even General Toombs. He hid in the gorge to get away from the Union soldiers who tried to arrest him after The Late Unpleasantness. Joseph LeConte has come many times to study our geology. But all that probably doesn't interest you."

"On the contrary, I would love to hear anything you wish to tell me. This is all so different for me, I find it fascinating."

Amelia giggled. "Sort of like how I would be in New York City."

She proceeded to point out animals and plants as they hiked, everything from a delicate white orchid called "monkey face" to roundleaf sundew, a rare carnivorous plant. Amelia explained that insects got stuck on the red leaves and were thus fated to be nutrients for their captor.

"Yuck." Grace wrinkled her nose.

Some ways down the path, a tiny trickle of water made the face of a rock protrusion glisten, and there Amelia stopped. Thank goodness. Grace breathed deeply, enjoying the pungent scent of earth and woods.

"See anything strange about this little cliff here?"

"No."

"Look closely." Amelia smiled.

Polite obedience overriding skepticism, Grace leaned in. A tiny head poked out from a crevice. "Oh!" The water ran right over the pointed nose, which exactly matched the hue of the moss.

"The green salamander. Their skin must stay moist if they're to breathe. I like to see how many I can count in one place."

Amelia's face glowed with the exertion of the walk. A simple face, not striking, it drew the eye just the same, her expressions enhanced by her enthusiasm for her homeland. Despite Amelia's sighing for the big city, Grace could not picture her staying in one for very long.

"Twelve! That's a record," exclaimed Amelia with satisfaction. "Well, let's go on."

When they neared the water, cool mists drifted in refreshing billows, dispelling the warmth of the day. They came to an overlook at the brink of the falls that made Grace quite dizzy. Above, the river seethed and raged like a boiling cauldron. Then, with an almost deafening roar, it tumbled through a narrow channel between high cliffs. Below, precarious-looking board-walks and cables helped visitors descend to the surprisingly calm pool at the base.

"Do you want to go down?" Amelia shouted.

The few people brave enough to do so received a drenching by the clouds of spray. Visions of plunging to her death came to mind. Vigorously, she shook her head.

Amelia laughed and pointed away from the falls. "Let's go a ways upstream, then."

As they beat their way toward the base of Tempesta Falls, Grace's staccato breathing and heartbeat and trembling legs revealed a painful lack of preparation for the rugged terrain. The extent of her exercise in New York had been on the ballroom floor, and that infrequently. While Amelia trudged ahead, she struggled to keep up, leaning heavily on her stick. Loose gravel rolled beneath her boots, and she grabbed for trees to pull herself along. At one point, Grace followed Amelia through a crevice in the rocks so narrow, she had to turn sideways.

"We've just threaded the Needle's Eye," Amelia said on the other side. "Some call it Lover's Squeeze."

Grace panted so hard she couldn't reply. One look at Grace's face caused Amelia to steer her toward a large flat rock away from the river.

"I'm sorry." She uncorked the canteen she had brought along and handed it to Grace. "How thoughtless of me. You seemed to be doing so well, but I should have known—"

"It's all right." Grace panted.

"We needn't go farther. Let's just rest here a bit." She produced two summer peaches from her skirt pockets and offered one to Grace.

Grace accepted. "I suppose I have a bit too much

pride to admit when I'm in over my head." Chuckling, she bit into the firm, juicy fruit.

"It's my fault. But what did you think of the falls?"

"Tremendous. Worth the hike."

"I agree. I always feel God's presence so strongly here. Maybe you do like it well enough to stay a while?"

Grace smiled. "We plan to stay the whole summer."

"Oh, there's lots to do, with all the activities the hotels offer, and there are definitely spots where the water is much more accessible. I'll also have to introduce you to some of the local young people."

"That would be nice. Thank you for wanting to take time with me."

Amelia's eyes rounded. "Just what I was thinking—about you. I'm not very exciting company for a high-society lady."

Grace shook her head. "But I'm not—for all my aunt's talk. I'm sorry she went on so at your father's soda shop. She can be a bit...pompous...at times. I was afraid she would completely put you off."

"I did find her talk interesting, if a bit—well, intimidating. And I doubt Professor Schmidt could be so easily discouraged. He seems quite intrigued by her. He's rather lonely, you know. I think he leaves his science lab and comes up here in hopes of meeting the right sort of woman."

"Oh." The teacher...attracted to her aunt? She had never given much thought to what she would do if Martha ever married. The idea had seemed so unlikely.

"Well, maybe he'll find a similar mind in that Professor Leon who's coming to The Grand View, whatever that is about."

"Professor Leon?" Amelia's dark eyebrows winged high above her blue eyes. "Don't you know? Professor Leon is not really a professor, he's an aerialist."

"A—what?"

"An aerialist. His real name is Mr. St. John. Mr. Young saw him walk between two buildings at Five Points in Atlanta and decided that bringing him up here would be just the thing to draw a crowd and make a buck. He's going to walk a rope strung across the gorge later in July."

Grace's mouth dropped open. She shuddered as she imagined such a feat, then the crowd Amelia had mentioned. "This place will be a madhouse." So much for peace and quiet.

Amelia nodded and wiped her mouth with her handkerchief, tossing her peach core into the woods. "People are coming from all around. Be glad your hotel room is secured for the summer."

"And I thought I was getting away from all the hoopla."

"Don't you like it? New York City, I mean? Your aunt certainly seems to."

Grace thought a moment, watching the turbulent river. After a couple of men with their shirtsleeves rolled up passed them, exchanging nods, she spoke. "Even my aunt has a love-hate relationship with the place." She laughed a little bitterly. "I think she just wants to show everyone that though she was forced to leave the South, she isn't beaten—that she's as good as they are. She hates depending on Yankee money, but she loves what it can buy."

"I take it your mother is deceased?"

"Yes, at my birth. Aunt Martha has been my caregiver ever since." She headed off Amelia's next question. "My father takes care of us financially but isn't very involved in our lives."

Thankfully, that seemed to satisfy her companion for the moment. Amelia cocked her head. "How did you come to be an opera singer?"

"My aunt noticed my voice quite early. When its quality did not dim in my early teens, she convinced my father I needed a tutor. He employed Monsieur LeMonte, himself once an opera star. Eventually, Monsieur found me parts in the chorus and as an understudy. Then a secondary role this past season. I'm afraid it rather went to Aunt Martha's head."

Even her father had warmed, sending her flowers and dresses, and of a finer quality than before. "We'll soon be eating watercress sandwiches and cakes from Dean's in Mrs. Vanderbilt's parlor," Martha had tittered. Grace's father's family had made their fortune with wise investments in mills, a successful newspaper, and railroad ventures. Dr. Hampton Galveston was now, along with his wife and their children, a permanent fixture on Caroline Astor's list of "The Four Hundred."

"It must have been amazing, singing to all those rich and powerful people, all their eyes fixed on you," Amelia mused in a tone of dreamy wonder.

Grace smiled somewhat sadly. "I admit, it had its charms. But..." How much should she say to this friend she had just met, but who was so easy to talk to? "I never did fit in with them. I'm much more comfortable here."

"Then I'm glad you're here. And I know you're on strict orders not to make a peep while you are, but maybe just once before you leave...I could hear you sing too?"

"Of course." It would be a pleasure to sing for such a genuine and appreciative person.

Finally. Grace felt ready for the return hike to the hotel. She and Amelia parted ways with a promise to play cards on the morrow. Grace dragged into the elegant lobby, her skirt hem muddy, her clothes dampened from perspiration and the mists of the falls, her hair straggling down, and her spirits higher than they'd been in months.

Aunt Martha, who sat with a cup of tea at a small table in the lobby, gasped in horror. "What in the world happened to you?"

"Aunt Martha, what did you think I would look like after hiking to Hurricane Falls?" Grace resisted rolling her eyes. "Could you please have a supper tray sent up to my room?"

34

"Well, you're certainly not presentable for the dining room. Merciful heavens!"

As tired as she was, Grace laughed as she climbed the stairs. She had Maureen draw her a warm bath and dump in a liberal dose of scented salts to soothe her aching limbs. Her supper tray arrived as Grace toweled off.

While dining on herb-encrusted mountain trout, long grain rice, and vegetables, she pondered what Amelia had said about sensing God's presence in nature. She had definitely been aware of a power today, and at the same time, a peace. Even though Maum Sally had sought to teach Grace about a loving Heavenly Father, Grace's experiences since, and even the somewhat stilted church services she attended, caused her to believe in a rather impersonal Creator. But maybe there was more to it than she had thought, for she sensed an opening in the heavens as it were, as if Someone benevolent suddenly smiled down on her.

One of the things missing in her life had been a friend. Someone to talk to in an open, unpretentious manner as she had to Amelia today. She *had* been bottling things up inside. More relaxed than she had been in months, she climbed between lavender-scented sheets and fell asleep the moment her damp head touched the pillow.

CHAPTER 3

*B*y the time the town celebrated the Fourth of July, Grace had been at The Cliff House for almost a week. During that time, she read and played cards with the elegant tourists chosen by her aunt, but Martha proved less understanding of Grace's preference for viewing L'Eau d'Or, Oceana, Bridal Veil, and Sweet Sixteen falls—and numerous cascades from feeder creeks. She and her new friend added ping-pong and tennis to their daily hikes. They even "took in the waters" at Indian Arrow Rapids, where the shallowness of the river allowed them to sit and let the current beat against their backs. The summer heat forgotten, they splashed and frolicked like children in their square-necked, scalloped-skirted bathing suits with bloomers.

The Fourth entailed a parade. Grace watched the procession from the front porch with her aunt, both of them enjoying ice cream the Mosses churned for their guests. Licking the creamy, homemade treat, Grace almost forgot the sweat trickling beneath her corset as they smiled and waved at brass bands, clowns and jugglers, children in small wagons with dogs yipping after them, the local fireman's association, and buggies bedecked with red, white, and blue bunting.

The local women always went to decorate the graves of their Confederate dead and picnicked after the ceremony. But as an outsider, Grace would never have thought of attending.

That evening, dressed in a short-sleeved bottle-green gown that bared her neck, she stepped onto the upper porch outside Aunt Martha's room. So far, she had avoided the dances in the hotel ballrooms, but tonight, Martha insisted Grace join the festivities. Grace would enjoy no peace until she did.

"There she is! What luck," called a familiar and welcome voice.

Below, Amelia stood on the side of the busy street, looking up at Grace. With her were two young men and another young woman. Grace waved.

"Look what we have—fireworks!" Amelia gestured to the bulging bag clasped by the dark-haired man at her side. Much more interesting to Grace, however, was the broadly smiling face above ... easily one of the most handsome she had ever seen. "Come, Grace. I promised to introduce you to some friends."

Grace leaned over the rail. "I'll be right down."

Not even pausing in Aunt Martha's bedroom, she

offered a hasty explanation and good night. She might not be going to the dance, but she *was* going out. Music blared on the ground floor. A carefree, nervous excitement flooded her.

The foursome waited for her next to the main door, Amelia dancing from foot to foot like a ten-year-old. The handsome man was Daniel Monroe, whose parents lived in Clarkesville. His father had ties to the local railroad and owned a woolen mill. The other gentleman, hardly shabby himself with his high cheekbones and blond hair, was Trent Hargrove, brother of Alice Hargrove. The aforementioned Alice pressed near Daniel as Amelia introduced Grace, turning her sweet face with rosebud lips up to him.

"Now let's find a place to set those off. I've been waiting *all day*."

Daniel glanced at Grace, his pained look a silent apology that they'd hardly had a chance to speak first.

She encouraged him by saying, "Yes, let's."

"Well, I guess the street's the best place. Let's go down a bit from the hotel, though."

With Amelia walking beside Grace, Alice chattering in Daniel's ear and clinging to his arm, and a whistling Trent bringing up the rear, they found a relatively quiet side street. Trent set down his lantern, which coupled with the moonlight gave Daniel enough illumination to unload his bag of goodies.

"Matches." He held out his hand.

Amelia complied.

Before Grace could prepare herself, something whined and exploded near the feet of the ladies, shooting off light. They all jumped and squealed with the required amount of surprise.

"Oh, you just *had* to scare us." Alice fanned her face. "Let's light the Chinese firecrackers."

Those created a great deal of noise, drawing a disgruntled old man to the porch of his nearby house.

Trent gave a lame shrug in the man's direction. "What's the Fourth of July without a few fireworks?"

Rather than confront them, the man went back inside.

Daniel brought out some wand-like shapes and gave one to Amelia. "These should make less noise. Once I light it, it will sparkle. But hold it at arm's length."

Daniel struck the match, and Amelia giggled as golden light spewed from the end. But the sparks so near their voluminous skirts made Grace's pulse race. When Daniel extended one to her, she hesitated.

"It will be all right." He offered an encouraging smile. "Dangerous as they appear, I've never known these to set anything afire."

She took the wand, and he lit it. Vibrant green fizzled from the end. She laughed, turning in slow circles like the other girls. The colors dazzled her eyes. When her dizzy gaze settled on Daniel, he was staring at her. A strand of his side-parted hair fell softly over his forehead. She smiled. He smiled back. Instant connection. She stopped short of analyzing that.

After they set off a couple of Roman candles, the balls of fire shooting high up into the air and drawing passersby, Daniel suggested they take a buggy ride. "That will give us a chance to get to know Miss Galveston," he said.

The traffic of tourists going from one end of town to the other, partaking of the many celebrations occurring simultaneously, clogged River Street. But the plentiful number of pleasure vehicles made it easy to hail a driver. As they climbed into the open carriage with facing seats, the man in the top hat asked, "Where to?"

"Just drive about, if you please," Trent told him.

The men sat on one side, the women on the other. Their skirts made it crowded, but Grace would have been too nervous had she been crammed in beside the dark-haired young man who now faced her. As it was, she struggled to keep her eyes off of him and remember that there were other people in the carriage.

"So how are you enjoying your stay in Tallulah?" Daniel asked.

"Very much, especially now that Miss Wylie has taken me under her wing." Grace smiled at her new friend.

"We've been having lots of fun. I broke her in the first day with the hike to Hurricane Falls." Amelia winked at her.

"You didn't." Trent groaned. "I don't even do that hike."

"I did! She complained less than you do. Oh, look,

Grace, there's the bank. I think I told you Alice and Trent's father manages it."

"No, you hadn't said."

"But she told us that you were an opera singer." Alice leaned her golden head forward and foxed her slanted green eyes on Grace. "Do you live in one of those huge mansions on Fifth Avenue?"

"Alice." Her brother nudged her skirt with his shiny shoe.

But Grace chuckled. "Hardly. Well, I have to admit my father does make his home in that area, but my aunt and I live in a modest brownstone fronting Gramercy Park. I have always lived there. My father remarried after my mother passed away."

"Oh." Alice's mouth turned down. "But...I thought Amelia said your family was of Southern stock."

"Yes, but I'm afraid there is not much left of my mother's side of the family." Grace bit her lip.

Daniel cleared his throat, then said brightly, "I've been to New York once, as part of my graduation trip. We even went to the opera. My mother is a huge fan. She made us wait to go until Christmas so she could see a performance. Of course, that was some years ago, when the opera was still housed in The Academy of Music."

"Ah, yes, I didn't begin until the new building was up. I remember being in awe of Christine Nilsson as Marguerite in *Faust*." Grace smiled. "After that, it's been nothing but Lilli Lehmann in German roles. But what else did you see while in New York?"

"The Metropolitan Museum of Art, of course." Daniel's eyes glowed with enthusiasm. "It was amazing."

"I agree. I don't care what all the people say who are mad that it keeps on expanding and crowding out Central Park. Of course, the park is one of my favorite places, too, but to me it seems not a detraction, but—"

"A complement!" Daniel finished her sentence.

"Yes, exactly."

He smiled in satisfaction. "There was an early freeze while we were there, and people were skating on the pond and sleighing through the park."

"I've always dreamed of a sleigh ride." Amelia sighed.

Grace grimaced. "I wouldn't know. Monsieur LeMonte will hardly let me outside in the winter. He's afraid my vocal chords will freeze." She laughed a bit tightly. "I have to be resigned to hearing the sleigh bells as they speed past."

"How sad." Was that a touch of sarcasm in Alice's tone?

"Tallulah is quite beautiful even in winter." Daniel gazed at a house with lavish gingerbread trim as they passed. "The ice and snow on the mountains. If I've seen New York in the snow, maybe one day, you'll get to see Tallulah Falls all covered in white." He smiled in a way that made Grace's heart flip.

"I'd like that."

"And we'd all like it if you'd come to our church on Sunday...Trinity Episcopal, up on the hill." He pointed. "Lots of the tourists go there."

"I don't see why not." Aunt Martha would certainly agree.

Alice, beginning to look petulant over her exclusion, took the opportunity to claim Daniel's attention, giving a description of the grave-decorating ceremony. She had taken roses and a flag to the grave of Major Somebody, probably her distinguished Confederate grandfather.

Grace bit her lip. She would not let Alice's comments about how moving it had been to honor their Southern defenders, and how *that* was what meant something to her about the holiday, bother her. They were passing The Robinson House, but Grace wasn't interested in the throngs of people surrounding the brightly lit inn. Instead, she turned her subtle attention to the man across from her.

Daniel Monroe intrigued her. His clothes were not new but were of good quality. His features were aristocratic, but he was so unaffected. His square jaw and straight brow spoke of strength of character, but his consideration of others showed a gentleness and keen perception that drew her. He was so very different from the dandies to whom she was accustomed, with their British-styled mannerisms—even different from Blake.

He had spoken so little of himself. Next time they met, Grace would be the one to ask questions.

~

They were going to be late. And it was all due to her aunt's lingering over her coffee.

Grace tapped her foot. "Aunt, we must go now." She flung her hand toward the open window. "There's the church bell."

With a sigh, Aunt Martha patted her lips with her linen napkin. Back in New York, Martha acted plenty sharp about morals and church attendance, but that was due in greater part to her desire to see and be seen than to any real religious devotion. While on vacation, she clearly felt there was no such need for posturing.

Grace was ready to throw all respect to the wind and head out the door without her when Aunt Martha finally rose and reached for her parasol. Outside, Grace set as brisk a pace as her skirts allowed, aiming for the small white church on the hill above. People were filing in. By the time they arrived, all the congregants had taken their seats.

"Hmm." Aunt Martha's tone showed surprised approval of the gracious interior.

Amelia and her family sat several rows up. No Daniel. Amelia turned and waved. But all the seats were taken save a few spots in the back. Grace and Martha slid into a pew.

"So," Martha whispered, "where is this young man you nearly broke my neck with haste getting here to see?"

Grace studied the crowd again. No, he definitely wasn't present. As the pianist began to play, her heart sank. And he had seemed so eager to meet her again!

Then a side door near the front of the sanctuary opened. Daniel! Prepared to overlook his tardy and unconventional entrance, she curved her lips into a smile of welcome. But he wasn't looking for her. He wore a white robe over his dark suit and carried a large Bible. Grace's mouth fell open in a most unladylike gesture as Daniel Monroe walked right up to the platform in front of the congregation and sat down in the big, carved oak chair.

CHAPTER 4

*D*uring the liturgy and singing on Sunday mornings, Daniel always availed himself of the opportunity to worship and prepare his heart to deliver the morning's message. His routine prayer focused on his decrease so the presence of the Lord might increase. This request proved necessary on a weekly basis in light of the half dozen, dewy-eyed teenage girls who never failed to line the front pew, and doubly—no, exponentially—so with the glorious red-haired angel present. This time, because of Grace, he asked for the proper focus for *himself.* The one direct glance at her he did sneak met with her raised eyebrow. Uh-oh.

During the hymn "This Is My Father's World," she did not sing but wrote something in a tiny notebook. Hmm.

Daniel concentrated on the message God had given

to him for that week. Some of those present would not warm to it. When he had been appointed to the newly built church here in Tallulah Falls, it had been with the understanding that it would draw not only the residents of the town, but wealthy vacationers as well. His background made him the ideal candidate to fill Trinity's pulpit. And in the last few years, he had found that the relaxed atmosphere of a summer retreat opened many tourists to spiritual truths. He counted on that today.

Standing at the pulpit, he directed the congregation's attention to Matthew 19:16-30, the story of the rich young ruler. The text which he read aloud detailed how that man had come to Jesus asking what he should do to receive eternal life. The fact that he had called Jesus "Good Teacher" had given the Lord the perfect opportunity to point out, "There is none good but one, that is, God." Then He had encouraged the young ruler to obey the commandments—avoiding adultery, lying, stealing, murder, and also honoring one's parents and loving one's neighbor. These things the ruler confirmed he had done.

"But he *knew* something was missing," Daniel told his listeners. "He knew the truth of what God had said, the lack of goodness within himself. For he asked, 'What lack I yet?'"

Some fashionably attired individuals, including Grace's aunt, shifted in their seats. But the eyes of most fastened on Daniel's face.

"Have you ever looked inside and known there was

an emptiness—and something holding you back from God? Jesus knew this young man's dilemma. For He replied, 'If thou wilt be perfect, go and sell that thou hast, and give to the poor, and thou shalt have treasure in heaven: and come and follow Me.' The Lord knew this was the one thing the man was unwilling to do, for he had allowed his money to tie him to earth and its pleasures. Thus, the young man went away sorrowful."

Daniel went on to share from the Scriptures how Jesus had explained to His disciples why the rich found it difficult to enter heaven, because one must be willing to leave homes, lands, and families, to take up one's cross and follow Him. He then clarified that wealth did not equate godlessness, for among his acquaintances were many blessed by abundance who loved the Lord wholeheartedly and shared with the less fortunate.

"Financial abundance can be a gift," he said, "rather like a Christian heritage—or the ability to lead—or a beautiful voice."

He smiled slightly, catching sight of Miss Galveston's brown eyes fixed on him.

"And like all gifts, it is at its greatest when used to the glory of God, and as He intends. The point the Lord made was that the issue lies with the attitude of our hearts. No possessions, no experiences, no talents, can fill the void created by the Lord. Nothing can but Himself. We must hold all other things in life lightly, placing them in subjection to His sovereignty, *willing* to let them go if need be. Realizing that fulfillment comes only through a personal relationship with Jesus."

Daniel flipped the pages of his well-worn Bible. "In closing, I'd like to share a verse from Proverbs 13—number seven." Slowly he read, "'There is that maketh himself rich, yet hath nothing: there is that maketh himself poor, yet hath great riches.'"

After the service, Daniel stood at the front door. He had removed his robe to appear less formal as he spoke to each departing parishioner. Grace Galveston and her aunt, having lingered in conversation with the Wylies, were among the last to exit. Even before he saw Grace's very intentional expression, Daniel knew what she would say. Taking Grace's proffered hand, he let manners fly to the four winds and headed it right off.

"I don't blame you one bit for what you're surely thinking of me, but before you write me off forever as deceptive and unfeeling, please allow me an opportunity to explain. Say, a stroll this afternoon?"

She chewed her full lower lip and contemplated him. He put all the little boy pleading into his face he could muster.

Before Grace could answer, her aunt edged forward. "Daniel *Monroe*? Not related to the Monroes of Darien, Georgia?"

He turned to the stately woman. "Why, yes, ma'am. And once again, I am sadly lacking in manners, for I should have—"

"Given me an opportunity to introduce my aunt, Martha Hampton," Grace finished for him.

"Yes."

He reached for Miss Hampton's gloved hand, intending to bow over it, but Martha gave a sniff and waved off his attempt. Then, unexpectedly, she tapped him with her parasol. "You shall join us for luncheon at The Cliff House and explain all." Up snapped the parasol, cloaking her in regal shade.

Her tone brooked no argument. Besides, she provided the exact opportunity Daniel craved. He jumped into motion. "Please give me just a minute to close up the church, and I'll escort you ladies to the inn."

"You were only an infant when the war began, and you had an older brother named James. Your parents were fine Christian people," said Martha over a fine congealed salad, as if having come to these conclusions as they strolled to The Cliff House and congregated at a table by a cliff-side window. "Having come from money, you at least have some entitlement to speak about the subject."

Daniel and Grace both stared at her.

"Well, don't look at me like I'm a soothsayer." She laughed. "All that is if my memory serves me correctly and your parents were indeed owners of a plantation outside Darien."

Daniel recovered. "It's true. In fact, my brother still lives there. The land is sharecropped now, but he stays busy overseeing things, including our own portion, and our small shipping business. But forgive me...I'm at a loss..."

"My father shared an informal acquaintance with yours. He was the owner of Hampton Hall outside Savannah. All the planter families knew the other planters and the cotton factors up and down the coast." Martha leaned to her right to allow a waiter to deliver the main course.

"Naturally, my memories of the war years are very few, really up until the time my father decided to cut most of his losses and move us to our summer home in Clarkesville. I was about six or seven then. But, yes...I do think Hampton Hall sounds vaguely familiar." Daniel paused, cocking his head to one side. "I believe my father once said it was a terrible shame that it was among those burned, for it was one of the finest on the coast."

"It was," Martha agreed in a thick voice, eyes on the meat she cut.

"And the land, is it still in your family?"

"Sold for back taxes." Martha's knife slipped out of her fingers and fell to her plate. She tightened her jaw. "This beef is far too tough. The roast at Del Monicoe's always melts in one's mouth."

Daniel frowned at the protein on her plate. "Cantankerous old cow."

Martha gave a quick bark of laughter that caused

Grace to look at her in amazement. It was probably a good idea to keep the conversation moving.

"Well, now I am more certain than ever about the invitation I already planned to extend today. I mentioned to Miss Galveston what an avid opera fan my mother is—and herself an accomplished musician. If she learned that I had made the acquaintance of a Metropolitan Opera singer and failed to bring her for a visit, I would never hear the end of it. And now, also knowing that our families have this connection...well, what do you ladies say? I had planned a visit home this week. Will you accompany me?"

A tiny frown of uncertainty flitted over Martha's face.

Grace's back stiffened. She had been patient and attentive during the exchange, but now her brow furrowed. "At this moment, I feel quite unprepared to answer that question, as I am still waiting to hear why you invited me to church but failed to tell me you were the minister."

"Uh...yes." How to share the truth without sounding immodest? Daniel tapped a finger on his unused dessert fork. "I'm very sorry about that. Well, sort of. You see, I was so enjoying the evening we met, and how naturally everything flowed. You know how when people find out you're an opera singer, things some-times change? Well, in a strange way, being a minister is rather similar. You let it out of the bag, and the next thing you know, people stop acting like themselves. Only, around me, they get all stiff and careful."

Grace's laughter pealed forth, a lovely musical sound that seemed to race down his spine like...like a finger over piano keys. He sat up straight in response and smiled. "I can imagine it might be like that," she said, nodding.

He grinned, letting out his breath. "Also...I didn't want you to come to the service because you felt obligated, invited by the minister and all."

At the implication of his words, the smile lingered about her lips. He gave the smallest nod in response to her searching gaze. Yes. He had wanted her to come because she had liked him and wanted to see him again.

Martha broke their little moment of connection by asking, "So if your parents live in Clarkesville and your church is here, where do you live?"

"I was a permanent boarder of Mr. Young's before his hotel burned. Oh, not The Grand View," he inserted quickly when their eyes widened, "the Young's Hotel, or The Tallulah. It sat on the upper gorge overlooking Indian Arrow Rapids. If you drive by the site now, you'll see it's being rebuilt. But I decided I needed something more—stable. I was able to find a small house in town for a good deal."

Thick slices of shortcake topped with cream and fresh strawberries arrived.

"Mmm." Grace picked up her fork.

But Martha sighed, leaning back in her chair. "Really, I don't think I can. After your stirring sermon, sir, that beef quite wore me out." She didn't laugh along with Grace and Daniel, but she appeared drained, not vexed. "I'd like a nap now. I think I'll retire to my room."

Daniel stood with her. "About that invitation . . ?"

The ladies glanced at one another. Grace nodded.

"Very well," said Martha. "We would be pleased to accept. I'll let you arrange all the details with my niece."

"Thank you, ma'am. My family will be delighted." He held out Martha's chair and caught her eye as she moved back from the table. "With your permission, I hoped to take Miss Galveston to see the view from Lover's Leap this afternoon. That is, if she is so inclined."

"Oh, wonderful." Grace brightened. "You can tell me the legend about the spot."

"That's fine. I'll send down our maid to accompany you. Good afternoon, Mr. Monroe...I mean, Rev. Monroe." Martha smiled stiffly. "My, that will take some getting used to. You don't look old enough to be out of college yet."

After the older woman had gone, Daniel sat back down. He enjoyed the sensation of being alone with Grace, watching her savor her dessert. Their solitude proved short-lived, though, for when he sallied into the lobby with Grace on his arm, a young maid waited there to follow them on their walk. At least she kept a discreet distance so that, while they were properly chaperoned, she could not hear everything they said.

"Of course, you know all these lands once belonged to the Cherokees," Daniel told Grace as they strolled south on the hotel grounds. She nodded. "Many stories have grown up from that time. It's said that the Cherokee rarely ventured into the gorge."

"Why not?"

"They held the area in awe. Some of them believed a race of little people known as Yunwi Tsundi inhabited it. They were supposed to live in caves and under the falls and kidnap women and children...who never returned."

"How strange." Her fingers tightened on his arm. "I love to hear Indian lore."

"Well, since you're encouraging me, there's another tale of a mysterious Indian maiden who led an infatuated warrior to a high cave. Strange supernatural things befell him. When he awoke in the forest, he could find no trace of the cave or the girl. When he returned to his people, he found he had been missing for many years. He didn't listen to the girl's warning to not talk about his experience. When he was questioned, he revealed it all. Right away, he fell ill and died within a week."

"My, you know a lot about these things, for a minister." Grace shot him a teasing glance.

Daniel set a slow pace as they descended the trail toward Lover's Leap, aware his companion still wore her Sunday finery. He grinned and helped her over a fallen log, a wonderful excuse to briefly hold her hand. "You can't live in these parts and *not* know. Now Amelia, she's homegrown. I don't have her bragging rights."

At Grace's questioning look, he explained. "Her folks have been in these parts forever. She's Scotch-Irish, English, and a drop Cherokee."

"*Really*?" Grace seemed fascinated, likely envisioning Amelia's glossy dark hair and high cheekbones. "That explains her bond to the land. It must be wonderful to have such a sense of belonging." Before Daniel could respond to the wistful lilt in her tone, she stopped walking as her gaze fell on a grouping of large boulders in the forest ahead.

"That's Council Rocks." Daniel tilted his head. "Ties in to the legend of Lover's Leap. They say many years ago, a young white hunter was captured and held prisoner there, where the Indians liked to meet. A beautiful Indian girl named—you guessed it—Tallulah—fell in love with him. But her father sentenced him to be thrown into the gorge from what's now called Lover's Leap."

"Let me guess again...she jumped after him?"

"Your romantic heart has discerned the truth, or should I say, the legend."

Grace laughed and paused. Up ahead, in a slight thinning of the trees, a young man about Daniel's age bent over a large black box secured on stilts—a tripod.

Daniel smiled at the wonderful timing and called out, "Hello, Walter!"

The man swung around to look at them. "Oh, hello, Daniel."

Daniel introduced Walter Hunicutt to Grace. Walter took her in with the blank look of surprise. He knew Daniel did not often go about with young women.

"Walter can often be seen with this camera of his, capturing images of our town and the gorge...that is, when he's not making his twig furniture or painting," Daniel explained.

"My, how talented you must be." Grace smiled at the man.

Walter shrugged. "Been thinking about doing a series of postcards."

"A wonderful idea," Daniel agreed. "Bet you'd sell a million. You just setting up here?"

"I'm ready to shoot the view from the leap."

"I take it you want it without people?"

Walter pursed his lips. "I had thought so, but not necessarily. People do make it seem real. I've already taken one from down the cliffs, showing the precipice itself. So I suppose the two of you would make good subjects, if you're interested."

Grace inched up to the overlook as he spoke. When she took in the sheer drop below, she shivered and hurried back a few steps, her hand at her heart. The men laughed.

Daniel's conscience twinged for manipulating Walter's good manners and turning what probably would have been a view of the gorge into a view of

DENISE WEIMER

himself and Grace. He whispered in Walter's ear, "Pay ya later."

Under his moustache, Walter grinned lopsidedly and waved aside his words. No doubt, he saw why Daniel would want to make the most of the opportunity. He backed up his large-format wooden dry-plate camera and directed them to stand with their backs to the gorge, Grace on Daniel's arm. Within moments, the photographer captured their images for eternity, together.

"Come by later this week and pick up the picture." Walter shook his hand.

Daniel thanked him. While Walter inconspicuously packed up his equipment, Daniel found a large rock for himself and Grace to sit upon. The maid chose another rock within view. Quietly, he said, "I hope your aunt was not too upset by our conversation at lunch."

"Why should she be?" Grace turned to him, her earrings dancing.

"Well, she wanted to know about my family, but then as we talked about the past, I could tell it was painful for her. I am curious about one thing, though, if you'll permit me..." He waited for Grace to nod. "How did she end up in New York City?"

Grace sighed. "I've heard the tale so many times, but it still wrings my heart. My grandfather was already very ill at the end of the war. Most of the slaves had left, and he had taken on too much physical labor for his age. Even after a fever left him weakened, he continued

58

at the pace of a much younger man. When the Yankees came and burned the house, it caused his demise. He died only days later in one of the cabins. My mother and aunt were forced to flee into Savannah. They had to stay with a cold-hearted great uncle who was none too pleased to have more mouths to feed."

She told him how Hampton Galveston arrived in Savannah in January of 1865, a young physician under the red-and-blue silk banners of the 131st New York Volunteer Infantry. While on duty in the beleaguered, captured city, he encountered a beautiful, red-haired girl weeping on the steps of the military hospital, unable to find any work. Something about her stirred both his pity and his passion. When his regiment mustered out of service in July, he took Louisa, along with her older spinster sister, Martha, and their maid, Sally, home to New York.

"But that was a mistake," Grace almost whispered, even though their chaperone opened a small book and began to read, paying them little heed. Daniel leaned forward, attuned to her emotions. She swallowed. "His wealthy parents raised such a commotion at the arrival of his penniless Rebel bride that he was forced to set up housekeeping in a modest brownstone. He supported them by his own earnings."

She stared at the tips of her boots. "Then, my mother died in childbirth, my father unable to save her. It demoralized him. His parents saw an opportunity for him to still make a brilliant society match, if he would but separate himself from the past and keep things quiet—"

"—Miss Galveston," Daniel interrupted. "You don't have to—"

"No, it's all right." She fluttered her hand at him. "There's no sense in being mysterious." She turned her moist caramel eyes upon him and laughed shakily. "But you might as well call me Grace if I'm telling you all this."

He made bold to take her hand. "I'm honored." Her fingers trembled ever so slightly, which did strange things inside his chest.

She continued, "So he moved back home. Soon after, he married and began another family. Ever since, he has financially supported my aunt and me, but we rarely saw him until—until recently. His parents passed away some time ago, and that along with his wise investments in newspapers and railroads means that money is now no issue for him."

Behind her words, Daniel sensed the hurt Grace seemed unable to articulate. How could a man virtually abandon such a lovely, innocent child? Had he no idea what kind of scars he could leave? Daniel wanted to take her in his arms but contented himself with patting her hand. He cleared his throat. "I—uh—do feel I understand much more now. Thank you."

She looked into his eyes, long and hard, as if searching for something, the moment made all the more powerful by her silence. He found himself wanting to give it, whatever she needed. Finally, she said, "I liked your sermon this morning."

He waited for further comment or question. When none came, he chuckled lightly. "Does that mean I'm forgiven?"

"If you promise to be utterly honest from this moment forward."

He could have made a joke about her binding a preacher to truthfulness. Instead, he said, "I do."

"I also liked the song." Taking Daniel by surprise and forcing him to release her hand—with more than a touch of disappointment—Grace jumped up and started toward the overlook. "I've heard it once before. I wrote down the words so I wouldn't forget them. They are so appropriate for this place. I just have to laugh at the Darwinists. How could anyone ever believe that all this just evolved?"

She gazed over the gorge, the breeze lifting her skirts and her amazing hair. How could anyone believe *she* had just evolved? Suddenly, she began to sing, and the sound—so clear, so pure—transfixed him.

> This is my Father's world, and to my
> listening ears
> All nature sings, and round me rings the
> music of the spheres.
> This is my Father's world: I rest me in the
> thought

Of rocks and trees, of skies and seas—
His hand the wonders wrought.

This is my Father's world, oh, let me
ne'er forget
That though the wrong seems oft so
strong, God is the ruler yet.
This is my Father's world: why should my
heart be sad?
The Lord is King: let the heavens ring!
God reigns: let the earth be glad!

When she finished, silence fell. Even the birds had
ceased their chatter. As her voice had spiraled into the
words, "This is my Father's world: why should my heart
be sad?" her tone held such hope, such wistfulness, that
his own heart squeezed tight. The God-gifted, profes-
sionally trained quality of that voice painted visions in
his head of the sparkling world of the opera and the city
from which she had come, and for which she was surely
destined. And now he had to remind himself of his own
words from earlier that day, about how people changed
when they knew certain things about you. He had
admired her character before being awestruck by her
voice.

Grace turned around, her hands clasped before her
chest, her cheeks flushed. "There, I did it."

"Uh—was there ever any doubt that you could?"

"Why, yes." With a swish of her bustle, Grace

walked toward him in a fashion illustrating her name. "You know I'm here to rest my voice, and that's no joke. A certain role last season—well, changed things. A great deal of pressure fell on me, lots of rehearsals, preparations for the fall. It started to tell on me. I lost my breathing. And my nerve. There was one particularly awful moment ... but I don't want to talk about that on this beautiful day." She gave a wave of her slim, elegant hand. "And well, here I am."

Despite his rampant curiosity, Daniel would honor Grace's hint that he should not dig further. In his eagerness to make her comfortable, he blurted the next thing on his mind. "I can't wait for my mother to meet you." Then he flushed like a schoolboy. How foolish that sounded.

But she rewarded him with another of those beautiful peals of laughter.

She amazed and fascinated him, one moment vulnerable and open, the next, seemingly untouchable. Had he ever been this intrigued by a woman? His mother *would* have questions. And he had much yet to learn about where Grace Galveston stood with God.

Lord, I really like this woman. I mean, I really, really like her. Help me to be wise.

As if his face betrayed the seriousness of his thoughts, Grace, too, sobered. "About that," she said. "What would you think of Amelia Wylie coming along?"

"Miss Wylie?"

"Yes, don't you think she would really enjoy an outing?"

"I—I guess so..." Grace and Amelia were fast becoming friends, clearly, but why did Grace need to invite her? Had he scared her off? Oh, well. Best to put a good face on it. He straightened and forced cheer into his tone. "We'll have a wonderful time."

CHAPTER 5

The morning of their overnight trip to Clarkesville, Grace spent more time than usual in front of the mirror. With Maureen's help, she created an elaborate coiffure. Clad in a traveling gown with a stand-up collar and dropped waist, hues of peach, tan and chocolate offering smart contrast in plaid and solids, she made her way to the depot. The light in Daniel's eyes when he saw her rewarded all the effort. Amelia, who waited beside him, gave Grace an excited hug.

Something about the Rev. Daniel Monroe had caused Grace to open up and talk about herself at their previous meetings, not something she easily did. That very vulnerability had provided the catalyst for her suggestion that they include Amelia's stabilizing presence on their little trip. And now, she determined to learn more about Daniel—before they arrived at his parents' home.

The train had just puffed out of the station when she said, "I'd love to hear what prompted you to become a minister."

"Prompted me? Why, I guess that would be—God." He grinned as the others laughed. "But to answer you more fully, I had an uncle who was a minister. When I was a child, he had a great deal of influence on me. Since I, like him, was a second son, my parents did not protest my decision when I told them I felt God's call on my life."

"You think they would have had you been the older son?"

Daniel fell silent for a moment. "It might have made things more difficult if James had resisted working in the family business. But my parents love the Lord, and I like to think they would have found a way for me to pursue my calling."

"Do you ever wish for a larger church, in a larger city?" Aunt Martha asked. Naturally, she'd wonder why anyone would choose to remain in the backwoods.

Daniel shook his head. "Tallulah is home. I can't see myself being anywhere else. Of course," he added with a smile, "God's plans and ours don't always match up. I hope I'll always be in step with Him, willing to go where He leads."

Aunt Martha's brow rose imperiously. "With that

outlook, you may end up in the Appalachian wilderness somewhere, or in Africa."

But Daniel only chuckled. "You could be right, ma'am."

Grace bit her lip, having no wish to reveal that her feelings on this particular subject ran more parallel to Aunt Martha's than Daniel's. While she did not live and breathe for New York City society like her aunt, she did enjoy its conveniences.

And how puzzling were Daniel's references to his relationship with God...as though God spoke to him openly and frequently. Grace couldn't imagine having a human father that involved in the details of one's life, much less a heavenly one. Somehow, she knew Daniel's comments did not betray braggadociosness, though. That just wasn't the way he was. And the way he was made her want to know more.

That brought Grace to her own motives. Clearly, she found Daniel attractive, so she must admit that she desired more than a summer friendship. At least, she thought she did. But Daniel had just said he had no desire to leave Tallulah, and her life was unfolding in New York. Everyone seemed to believe that life should include the cultured Blake Greene. But he seemed so far away right now, and Daniel was so near, his handsome face turning toward her with the most heart-stopping smile. She would put the "buts" and "ifs" far from her and merely enjoy this interlude.

She smiled in return. "Is James your only sibling?"

"Oh, goodness, no. You mean, I've entirely failed to mention my sister?"

Grace nodded. Amelia giggled.

"I'm hoping you can meet her at dinner tonight, along with her husband and daughter."

"You have a niece?"

"I do." Daniel glowed as if he had something to do with this amazing fact. "Her name is Melanie. She's two years old. My sister's name is Emily Anne."

"Her husband, Mark Taylor, is a judge," Amelia added.

The train began to slow.

"We're approaching Clarkesville. The depot is a bit of a ride from the town, and my parents' home, so they will have sent a carriage," Daniel told them.

"That's a relief." Grace didn't want to sound whiny, but the July morning had begun to heat up, making the inside of the passenger car quite stuffy. She gave a subtle tug at the neck of her dress, trying to separate it from her sticky skin. "I'm unaccustomed to this southern humidity."

"Yes, it's a foe to be reckoned with even near the mountains." Daniel picked up the coat he'd shed.

As they disembarked the train, Grace's steps faltered at the sight of a grand open carriage drawn by two gleaming black horses, sporting a family crest on the side. Even Aunt Martha looked impressed. A somber Negro man stepped down from his perch to open the vehicle's door for them. "Mornin', Mist' Daniel," he said.

Daniel grinned at him warmly as he handed the ladies up. "Good to see you again, Abe."

Once their valises were loaded, they set off at a leisurely pace, parasols shading them from the sun. Daniel had their driver take a round-about route to allow them a brief tour of the town. Clarkesville exuded quite a different feeling from Tallulah. Tallulah's appeal came from its newer buildings and, of course, the mountain views and gorge. If Grace had not known better, she would have guessed that Clarkesville nestled in the heartlands rather than perched on the edge of the Appalachians.

Mature trees shaded grand antebellum homes set back among green lawns. Daniel pointed out several with comments such as, "Minis Hall, 1848," and "Gloaming Cottage, built by Jarvis Van Buren, a cousin of the past president...and the second story was added about 1870." Daniel explained that Van Buren had overseen the building of both the Presbyterian Church and Grace Episcopal Church. As they passed this lovely white structure with its tall, green-shuttered, multi-paned windows, Daniel told them that his family had long rented a box pew inside.

A plethora of hotels crowded the town square. Clarkesville had been considered the "jumping off" point for visitors to Tallulah and also to Toccoa Falls before the railroad had been completed. Grace glimpsed a brick courthouse on the town square before they turned up another side street.

"And at last...Crown Pointe." Daniel gestured ahead as they entered a narrow drive between brick pillars. "My father named the house, saying it was the jewel in the crown of all he owned, mainly because it was always the family's favorite retreat."

Grace leaned forward and gasped. "Why, it's beautiful!"

"It reminds me of Hampton Hall," said Aunt Martha in a strangled voice. Tears glistened in her eyes, and her face twisted as she struggled to contain sudden emotion. "Grace, this is much the sight that would have greeted you near Savannah, had our home been standing."

Imagining how Aunt Martha must feel, Grace ventured to place her hand over her aunt's. To her added amazement, Martha did not withdraw.

"How I wish..." she whispered.

The appearance of a couple on the front porch—Daniel's parents—turned Grace's attention. They waved, and as Daniel waved back, Grace and Amelia followed suit. The carriage drew up right in front of the house. As Grace alighted and mounted the steps between the two middle columns, she had a keen taste of what the life of the Southern aristocracy had been before the war...a life that had once been Martha's. She took her aunt's arm, understanding her a little more.

"Miss Hampton, Miss Galveston, may I present my

parents, Mr. and Mrs. William Monroe. Father and mother, I'm pleased to introduce Miss Martha Hampton, her niece, Miss Grace Galveston—and of course, you know Miss Wylie."

Grace held her skirt for a careful curtsy. Funny, how much she wanted these people to think well of her. She glanced up at a knowing smile on the lovely older woman's face, framed by reddish-brown hair swept back into a simple, old-fashioned style. Tiny creases marked the corners of Mrs. Monroe's eyes, but her bustled gown emphasized a still-trim figure.

Daniel's dark good looks came from his father, although a liberal amount of gray now sprinkled Mr. Monroe's hair and moustache. Of the two, the elder man was slightly the shorter. He bowed to the visitors.

Mrs. Monroe took Aunt Martha's hand, then Grace's. "We are so happy you've come to visit. I've been able to think of nothing else since Daniel told me of you. And of course, Miss Wylie, your company never fails to be a delight." She turned to the blushing young woman and gave her cheek a quick kiss.

"Thank you for having us," said Aunt Martha somewhat stiffly.

"Crown Pointe has reminded Miss Hampton of her girlhood home near Savannah," Daniel mentioned with a gentle smile.

"Ah, yes! Of course, Daniel told us about that. I can't wait to talk about it all. We'll show you to your rooms, then I thought we could have luncheon on the veranda.

The breeze makes it cool there, even most summer afternoons."

Inside, a curving staircase rose from a spacious entrance hall and wrapped around a brass chandelier. As they ascended, Mrs. Monroe explained that they could offer two guest rooms, one with twin beds. She asked if this would be comfortable.

"Why, yes." Amelia grabbed Grace's hand and drew her into the sun-kissed twin bedroom done in whites and greens that Mrs. Monroe showed them. Something told Grace only the polished presence of Daniel's mother kept Amelia from plunking down on a bed to test the mattress. Instead, she ran to peek out the window, then whirled around with a smile.

Grace drew her hand into the folds of her skirt, more uncomfortable over her new friend's show of affection than her enthusiasm.

"This will be delightful. It will give Grace and I time to get to know each other better, and Aunt Martha a bit of privacy. That is, if it suits you?" Amelia's sparkling eyes appealed to both of them.

"Certainly, Miss Wylie," Aunt Martha agreed, then pressed her lips together, doubtless in an attempt to not reveal quite how appealing the suggestion did sound.

"Yes, of course," Grace said. "Thank you, Mrs. Monroe."

"You're most welcome." Their hostess touched Aunt Martha's arm. "Miss Hampton, please call me Evelyn."

Aunt Martha flushed. "Martha."

As the older women departed for Aunt Martha's room, Amelia wasted no time shutting the door and leaning against it with a giggle. "Aren't his house and family wonderful?" she whispered. "I told you."

Grace nodded, though her stomach twisted. Did Amelia's praise stem from future hope for herself or for Grace? As often as she had longed to giggle and whisper secrets at bedtime with a sister or friend, she had no idea how to go about such confidences. In such unfamiliar circumstances, she was liable to make an awkward, awful mess of things—with both Amelia *and* Daniel.

CHAPTER 6

*O*ver a cool, elegant lunch, conversation centered on common acquaintances, shared past events, and the pleasures of Martha's and Grace's visit in Tallulah. Then, as the ladies walked shrub-lined paths and admired Evelyn's rare rose varieties and Cherokee apple trees from the Van Buren nursery, their hostess wanted to hear details of their lives in New York.

The congenial atmosphere continued after they rested, Grace changed into an ice-blue taffeta moiré dinner dress, and they gathered again for supper. Judge Taylor arrived with his family around five. Two-year-old Melanie hurtled herself into Daniel's arms and squealed as he tossed her into the air.

Grace watched the exchange, smiling.

"I'm afraid she's a little wound up," Emily Anne, whose intricately rouchéd peach silk gown appeared as well-made as Grace's New York creation, apologized. "She was so excited about seeing 'Uncle Danny' today that she wouldn't take her nap."

"We're hoping the excitement continues to over-power crankiness," Judge Taylor added wryly, dropping his walking stick into a brass container near the door. He cut a fine figure in his black frock coat.

"Oh, dear." Daniel held the child out like a ragdoll. "No nap? You won't get cranky, will you?" The little girl shook her head and pursed her cherubic lips for a kiss. Grace laughed as Daniel gave them a loud smack. "Never!"

Servants trundled the adorable but now tearfully protesting child off to have her meal in the kitchen as the adults filed into the dining room. There, candles gleamed on a Chippendale table set with white roses and silver. Efficient servants hastened in the first course and served it on Mrs. Monroe's blue-and-white floral china.

"These plates are lovely." Martha touched the thin edge. "1820s Spode Filigree. How did you come to save so many of your holdings, your possessions? I remember hearing black Union troops burned Darien to the ground in June of 1863, well before Savannah's demise."

"They did, indeed." Mr. Monroe frowned at the pork loin set before him. "Not an event my family will ever forget."

Mrs. Monroe leaned forward to allow a servant to deliver a serving of green beans. "Mr. Monroe was not at home, of course. He had always been a member of The McIntosh Light Dragoons, which eventually became The First Battalion and then part of the 5th Regiment, Georgia Cavalry." A trace of pride laced her words.

"I served on the coast for quite some time before we were shipped to Mississippi under Wheeler. Wounded in the Atlanta campaign," he added, flexing his arm, "and can still feel the effects of that. I was mad as fire to be laid up in the hospital there while Sherman razed our state and turned back to take Savannah."

"Anyway, dear, the burning of Darien..." Mrs. Monroe redirected.

"Yes, of course, go ahead."

Evelyn Monroe looked at Martha. "Our home was spared because it was occupied by Yankee officers."

"Oh!"

"Do you remember, Daniel? Emily Anne?"

"I hid him in the coal hole when they first rode up," Daniel's sister said.

Daniel snorted. "Thank you so much." Mock indignation firmed his reply. "I nearly choked to death— much less a glorious way to perish than at the hand of the Yankees."

"I was trying to be helpful."

"So you do remember?" his mother asked.

He nodded. "Only vaguely, though. After being

rescued from the coal hole, I remember having to stay in one of the tabby houses while the Yankees were there, and everybody acting calm and saying we must be very polite. But I could tell y'all were scared to death."

Mrs. Monroe sighed. "That we were."

"And angry. They could see the smoke of Darien fifteen miles away on St. Simons," Mr. Monroe told them. "The amazing thing is, like Atlanta, she's recovered. Goes to show our resilience as a people. Where once we shipped out cotton, now we're one of the largest lumber shipping ports on the southern coast."

"And thus, your shipping business, directed by your son James, still flourishes," Grace concluded with a smile.

"That, along with Mr. Monroe's business investments locally, have kept us from the genteel poverty to which so many of our friends were reduced." Mrs. Monroe smiled at her son. "During the off-season, Daniel helps his father oversee the mill."

Mr. Monroe forked a bite of squash. "Many of the people who built summer homes in this area had to sell them. Things have not been the same since."

"Fortune has truly been with you." Grace took a bite of her roll.

"Not merely fortune, Miss Galveston, but as we see it, the Lord's blessing." Mr. Monroe replied. He bowed his head slightly. "If you'll forgive the contradiction."

Grace did feel somewhat belittled, as if he pointed

out her lack of spiritual insight. Something rose within her. "Was it also the Lord's blessing that caused your prosperity before the war...or was it the labor of your slaves?"

Aunt Martha turned bright red. "Please forgive her. She's spent her whole life in a Northern city and has no idea how things were in the South."

Grace looked down at her plate, righteous anger battling with embarrassment. Even if she was right, she had spoken rudely to Daniel's father, her host. She could not bear to look at Daniel.

William Monroe held up his hand. "No, indeed. I'm sure I sounded more pompous than I meant to. And what Miss Galveston asks now centers on the best question of this century. As I'm sure you know from our son"—he glanced at Daniel—"we are a Christian family. I did inherit my father's slaves. I always believed in gradual emancipation, that a slow process could best equip the black race with the skills necessary to live as free people in society. But while I owned them, no matter how good a relationship we had, or how benevolent a master I was, even teaching them Christianity, my conscience could not rest. In my heart, I knew I permitted an inexcusable wrong. I only knew peace after the war, which it seems God used to bring about His own will."

"His own will?" Martha asked in a choked voice. "For so many innocent people to suffer and die, to be dispossessed?"

"Oh, dear. Now we've caused both of you upset. We must seem heartless to go on so, in light of your experiences, Miss Hampton." Mrs. Monroe's eyes filled with tears of compassion.

"God can use even the most disastrous of events. I think that is what my father meant." Daniel laid his hand on the table. "And *that* touches on perhaps the greatest question of all time—why God allows suffering. Of course, as I'm sure we all know—but still at times forget—it's that He allows humans a choice. Because of that, there is evil in the world. But difficulties can produce character, if we allow."

"Now we've done it." Emily Anne groaned, rolling her eyes as she raised her napkin to her lips. "We've gone and got him preaching. Mother's lemon layer cake will go completely unappreciated."

"It's my fault." Grace's shoulders sagged.

But Daniel smiled at her. "Nonsense."

Judge Taylor balled up his napkin. "I, for one, stand ready to appreciate cake."

Everyone broke into laughter, the tension dispelled.

After they finished the meal, Mrs. Monroe aimed to extend the renewed good cheer by shooing them into the parlor. She asked if Grace might sing something for them. Penitent for the dinner discussion and touched by William Monroe's humble words, she agreed before Aunt Martha could speak. To her surprise, Daniel slid onto the piano bench with a flourish and started thumbing through a music book.

Grace gaped at him. "You play?" Was there no end to his talents?

"A bit. Not like my mother, but good enough for... oh, 'Rose of Killarney,' if that suits you."

Grace nodded. That would hardly be a strain.

Emily Anne clapped her hands. "Oh, this is so exciting. I've never heard a real opera star before."

"Not a star—" began Grace.

"A *star*." Daniel's firm contradiction left no room for argument. His eyes met hers, and she flushed.

"You've sung for Daniel?" Amelia blinked at them. "When? I missed it?"

Daniel shrugged as if to downplay the event. "We took a walk after church, and she was so inspired by my preaching that she burst into song."

Grace play-hit his shoulder.

"And what a song it was." He pretended to reel drunkenly.

"Just a hymn from the service." Grace glanced back over her shoulder, even more embarrassed to confirm that Mrs. Monroe watched them with a measuring and thoughtful expression.

Daniel's fingers rippled over the keys. She sang the first verse by herself, easily capturing every note, then Daniel surprised her again by joining her in a rich baritone.

> My heart is a nest that is robbed and
> forsaken

When gone from my sight is the girl that
I love!
One word from your lips can my glad-
ness awaken,
Your smile is the smile of the angels
above!
Then meet me at twilight beside the
bright waters,
The love that I've told you, I'd whisper
once more;
Oh, sweetest and fairest of Erin's fair
daughters,
Dear rose of Kilarney, Ma-rour-neen
Astore!

Those gathered burst into applause. Daniel's gaze so distracted Grace that she hardly noticed. Mrs. Monroe reclaimed her attention when she said, "At lunch, you were telling us how you were trained in the *bel canto* technique, Miss Galveston."

"Yes." Grace smiled at her.

"Would you feel up to something a bit more challenging?"

"What did you have in mind?" Grace didn't dare look at Aunt Martha. How could she deny their hostess, Daniel's mother?

Mrs. Monroe rose with grace and fetched another music book. "Whenever we travel, we sometimes get to attend an opera. After I go, I buy the music and play it over and over. This is one of my favorite arias, from *Aïda* —when Aïda is so torn between her homeland, her father—and the man she loves."

Grace's heart plummeted to her feet. She stared with parted lips as Mrs. Monroe shooed Daniel from the piano bench. She knew the story of Aïda, the Ethiopian slave of Amneris, daughter of the king of Egypt, all too well. Aïda falls in love with the captain of the Ethiopian guard, Ramses, even though he is an enemy to her people and her mistress is set to marry him. Maybe Grace had always loved the story so much because of the way Aïda's father came to rescue her— her father, the king of Ethiopia.

Aunt Martha sat up straight. "Grace, you should not. The very role we're hoping for this fall, the very song you—you—"

"Botched in front of the most important people in New York's world of opera?" she finished in a faint voice. "Including the Vanderbilts."

"Oh, my dear, I didn't know." Mrs. Monroe's hands fell to her lap.

Martha continued to address Grace. "You're not ready. You're on strict orders to not tax your voice."

Mrs. Monroe moved to close her book, but Grace stayed her hand. "No, please, I *want* to. Wasn't I saying earlier how your mountain air has been working wonders?" She tried to make her smile convincing. She might as well face this sooner rather than later. Maybe if she could sing this aria here, in front of the most favorable crowd possible, she could put the awful memory to rest. She turned from her aunt, who was wringing her hands, to Evelyn Monroe, who looked askance at her. Grace nodded.

As the dramatic, tumbling piano notes began, she remembered that day in late spring when her father sent the invitation to a rare dinner at his home, along with a note. *This will be a gathering of opera supporters. Be prepared to sing. Go to Watkins for a new dress. Spare no expense. Charge to my account.*

She had done so, and the golden creation she purchased helped lend her confidence, even when her father's son and his Worth-clad wife coldly ignored her, and her half sister had snuck curious glances at her as if she were a circus performer. She could never have told her father ahead of time that Monsieur LeMonte's intensified lessons, her aunt's pushing, and most especially her father's own expectations—which he suddenly had begun expressing—had been causing her sleepless nights and difficulties singing. They all expected her to show herself worthy. And what didn't she have to justify? Her father's money, her mother's life, Aunt Martha's wasted years, even her own existence. Yes, all those things she held inside her, and their raw edges scraped when they stirred.

During dinner, a debate arose between Anton Seidl and several of the other men. Hungarian Seidl, personal friend to Richard Wagner, served as the new music director for the Met. They contended whether *Aïda* possessed a more Wagnerian or Verdian form, and should be performed in its original Italian, or in German.

"Well, let's just hear it both ways, and then we can decide...if Miss Galveston will humor us." Seidl, and then all at the long elaborate table, turned to her.

But of course she would. This was her chance, her moment. It was as good as an audition.

Yet more trepidation than excitement filled her when she stood in her father's parlor, ready to sing. The faces spun around her—her aunt's pinched, her father's imperious. She recalled the few times her father visited her as a child, how she had been dressed up and paraded, yet always too nervous to connect with the aloof man. It had been like that, only far more awful, for it was public. She couldn't get her breathing right. Panic surged. She fought it down. Her voice came out stiff, shallow, and when she cracked a high note, she could no longer bear to look at him.

"I'm—I think I need to sit down," she said at the end.

There had been no German version that night.

And now, Grace sensed an opportunity to turn a corner, inspired by these wonderful people surrounding her. Her voice emerged clear and pure as she began. "*Ritorna vicitor! E dal mio labbro uscì l'empia parola!*"

Her audience sat motionless. She closed her eyes, remembering why she had once enjoyed singing, letting the music and emotions swirl around her, building. Evelyn's fingers created beautiful trills interspersed with heavy chords. As the aria culminated with the hauntingly beautiful *"Numi, pietà"* passage—"Gods, have pity on my suffering! There is no hope in my woe. Fatal love, tremendous love, break my heart or let me die!"—Grace knew she could not have given a better performance.

The room fell silent. Totally silent. She looked around for an expression, a word. They stared at her. Amelia's mouth hung open. Martha held a trembling hand over her heart.

Then, from the next room where Emily Anne had laid Melanie when she fell asleep, came a tiny cry. "Mommy?"

Everyone burst into laughter. Emily Anne scurried out to get her daughter.

"Oh, dear." Grace covered her cheek with her hand. "My impassioned aria woke her up."

"My dear, never mind that. I'm afraid you have us quite speechless," Mrs. Monroe said. "Never have our walls been privy to such incredible music."

"You are a prodigious talent." Judge Taylor stepped forward to bow over Grace's hand.

"Thank you." Even as she accepted the compliment, she couldn't help herself. She glanced at Daniel.

He shook his head and repeated quietly, "A star."

Grace took a deep breath, feeling suddenly tired...
but happy.

Emily Anne noticed the gesture as she re-entered
holding Melanie. "Daniel, you should take Miss Galveston out to get some fresh air."

Daniel rose, but a rumpled head popped up from
his sister's arms.

"Uncle Danny!"

Clearly torn and not wanting to hurt the child,
Daniel looked back and forth. Emily Anne settled the
issue by announcing firmly that "Uncle Danny" had to
be a nice host and Melanie could see him the next day.
Daniel kissed his niece and offered his arm to Grace,
escorting her into the garden. The sweet fragrance of
roses and the nighttime humidity closed around them.

Grace turned to her companion. "I did it, just like at
Lover's Leap. You must be my good luck charm."

"Are you ready to take me with you and return to
New York?"

She laughed, then said seriously, "No. I don't want to
go back yet. You can't imagine how horrible it was the
last time I sang that aria. Worst of all...disappointing
my father." Her voice, and expression, fell.

Daniel put a finger under her chin to lift it. "It seems
your father expects much but gives little."

"He doesn't view our financial support as little." Her
eyes sought his.

Daniel's mouth tightened. "I'm not speaking of

money. A child's physical needs should be met as a matter of course, lovingly, not as a begrudged duty, or in proportion to the child's performance. And as to emotional needs..."

"I've learned not to expect the impossible. My father just isn't like that." Her voice now sounded small.

"Mine is."

"I know. I see..." She gestured to the home, with its lights gleaming within. "Your family is wonderful, gracious."

"I meant my Heavenly Father. And yours." He studied her intently. "Or do you think God is as distant as your own father?"

"I..." Grace could not meet his gaze. Instead of answering, she whispered a confession, hoping to turn the conversation away from the uncomfortable subject of God. "I left him a message at our house, before we came here, you know. Telling him where we were. All he has to do is inquire with our footman, who has the address of The Cliff House. I keep checking for a letter or a telegram, but..."

"None come," Daniel finished for her.

"He won't come either. It's idealistic of me, I know, hoping he might just show up, like Aïda's father—come to redeem me." She laughed lightly.

Daniel's large hand cradled the side of her face, startling her, snapping all her senses to full alertness in the thick, liquid stillness of the summer night. She sought his eyes, yearning, as usual, for the gentleness, the understanding, she found there. She leaned into his hand. His face, his lips, looked finely chiseled in the moonlight. Grace trembled. Would he kiss her?

But then his expression changed, as if a thought had just come to him. "Only God can redeem us. Do you know what I mean, Grace?"

The use of her given name softened his spiritual turn of mind only a little. She drew back ever so slightly, and he dropped his hand. "Why, yes." After all, she went to church all the time, and hadn't Maum Sally drummed the love of Jesus into her all during her childhood?

Daniel let out a soft breath. "I'm just afraid you're carrying around hurt inside you that you don't have to. The Lord 'relieveth the fatherless and widow.' Whatever hole your father has left in your heart, Jesus can fill."

"You sound like Maum Sally," Grace said, then choked on an unexpected lump of tears.

"Your mother's mammy?"

Grace nodded. What was he doing to her, gently unwrapping all her protective layers? Another one peeled away as he pulled her into his arms and laid his chin on top of her head. Her hands were trapped against his chest, and his heart thumped beneath her ear. Her own clamored much too fast for a comforting hug.

"She talked a lot about God?"

Again Grace nodded. Never had she felt more secure, but at the same time, such a jumble of confusing feelings washed over her that she raised her hands to her face to withhold tears. Unfortunately, that caused Daniel to release her and search for a handkerchief. She covered her face with it as Daniel waited in patient silence.

Grace exclaimed, "I'm sorry, I don't know what's wrong with me. I'm a mess tonight."

Daniel rubbed her bare arm, sending tingles skittering all the way to her slippers. "No need to apologize. It's been a long day, and I know that performance roused some emotion. Maybe some sleep will help."

She allowed him to lead her to the foot of the stairs in the entrance hall. Quiet voices still carried from the parlor.

"I'll make your excuses." He smiled.

"Thank you." She waited uncertainly, but he did not release her hand.

"Good night, my dear Grace." With those intent eyes fastened on her, he raised her fingers to his lips in a slow and purposeful movement and kissed them.

Half an hour later, Grace stood looking out the window in her bedroom when the door opened and Amelia entered. Grace admitted aloud, "I'm falling in love with him."

"What?" Amelia gasped, shutting the door.

Grace turned, her long white nightgown swirling

around her bare feet. "It's true, I am. What do you think of that?"

Amelia stared a moment, then gave a sudden deep chortle. "I think Alice Hargrove will soon be sinking her claws into you. She's had her eye on Daniel since before I can remember."

"Has he...does he care for her, or someone else, perhaps?"

Amelia shrugged. "Lots of girls set their caps for him, but he's never responded. It's as though he's...waiting."

"What about you, Amelia?" She had to ask.

"Me? What about me?"

"Yes." Grace twisted her fingers in her gown. "You and Daniel would make a perfect match. You have so much in common."

"What will you do if he turns out to care for you in return? Would you actually stay here?" Amelia drew closer.

"I don't know. I don't know! It's crazy—and I don't have any answers, only feelings—and who knows if it's not all just in my mind, anyway? But wait...you never answered *my* question." Grace fixed her friend with a suspicious stare.

Amelia sat on the bed and sighed. "Well, I'd be lying if I said Daniel didn't turn my head, or there weren't periods of time in the past when I had a crush on him. But that's all it ever was, just daydreams. And I can tell you, it's not all in your head. Daniel's never looked at me, or anyone, the way he looks at you."

Amelia's observation ignited a searing flame of hope in Grace's chest, doused just as quickly by sudden fear. For had she not sensed his reserve as much as she'd sensed attraction? A reserve that had to do with more than the fact that she lived in New York and he lived in Tallulah Falls.

CHAPTER 7

"*Y*ou're going *where*?" Aunt Martha stood in the doorway of Grace's bedroom with her arms akimbo.

"To see Aunt Fannie, the famous hostess of Sinking Mountain." Grace placed her second-most plain dress in a valise along with her personal effects. She wore her plainest dress, having left off her bustle frame under-skirt, and had arranged her hair in a simple knot. "Don't worry, Aunt, they've been there many times, and it will only be for a night or two."

"And you're traveling seven miles on bumpy back-roads in a wagon—to arrive uninvited at the house of a woman you've never even seen?" Martha looked at her as if she were losing her mind.

"It's not unusual, Aunt Martha. Parties from Tallulah go there all the time. They say the food and hospitality are worth the ride, and Aunt Fannie wants the company to come. Amelia says she had eleven children—ten daughters!—and as they've grown up and married, she's trained local girls to help serve all the visitors."

"She must have a large house."

"Actually, a log cabin." Grace snapped the valise shut.

Finally, Martha put her foot down. "Are you crazy? What would make you want to do this? It's time I step in and forbid such foolishness."

Forbid? Grace had not thought it would come to that. She put on her most winsome expression. "But Aunt, it's growing so crowded here, with Professor Leon's walk happening at the end of the week. Some of my new friends decided it was the perfect time to enjoy the peace and quiet of the country, and I want to spend time with them. Next month, we're going home. We'll be back plenty early to see Professor Leon cross the gorge. And meanwhile, Professor Schmidt and Mrs. Wylie want to take you to tea at Pine Terrace with the Mosses—and to dinner at the Wylies'. You'll hardly be alone."

Aunt Martha pursed her lips at the mention of the professor, who continued to ply her with attention. She had also taken a liking to their hostess, Mrs. Moss, a sensible, gracious lady near Martha's own age with gentle dark eyes and a sweet smile. "Well..."

"If you still have doubts, you could speak with the

professor. He will assure you this is a perfectly legitimate adventure."

"You've been spending an awful lot of time with that reverend." Her aunt cocked her head.

"I've hardly seen him in three days." Which was the main reason she was so eager to set out this morning, though she would hardly say so to Martha. "Besides, you liked his family."

"They're quality people, I admit, but have you given no thought to Blake Greene?"

Grace paused. In fact, she hadn't. Daniel Monroe had filled her mind, thoughts of him flitting in and out on a constant basis. Even yesterday, when she and Amelia stood at the gorge rim and watched Professor Leon swim across the river far below, grasping the rope he would walk from Inspiration Point, one of the highest outcroppings, to Lover's Leap, on July 24. Workers arranged an intricate network of support ropes to secure the main line.

"Alice has stewed ever since Daniel invited you to Crown Pointe," Amelia told Grace. "She's using the number of people around here as an excuse to get up an outing to Aunt Fannie's. She figures at best you won't go because the trip is so arduous, giving her time alone with Daniel—and at worst, you will go, and she'll be able to make you look bad by demonstrating your poor endurance of hardship."

"Of all the nerve." Grace had huffed. And obviously, she'd made her mind up right then. "But why is Daniel going? It seems as though this would be a prime opportunity for him to mix with the people—you know, be an influence, invite them to church..."

Amelia nodded. "Yes, that's why we've seen little of him these past days. But Alice knows he has a weak spot for visits to Mrs. Smith's, and it's been ages since we've gone. Mrs. Smith is a Baptist, but she and Daniel have great appreciation for one another."

"You ought to think of Blake Greene," repeated Aunt Martha with more firmness, drawing Grace's mind back to the present. "When you next see him, after this separation, I have little doubt that he'll be ready to speak of very serious matters. If you go—if I agree—you must consider *that* on your visit to the country."

"I will, Aunt Martha." She'd consider it for one full moment.

Martha sighed. "Very well, be off with you. And if you don't return *at least* by day after tomorrow, I'm sending a search party out after you."

Grace laughed, confident she was in safe hands. She kissed her aunt's cheek. "Why don't you come down and wave us off? No doubt, Professor Schmidt is reading his newspaper in our lobby."

She enjoyed seeing straight-laced Aunt Martha grow flustered. But her aunt rose and followed her downstairs. There, as predicted, the said gentleman greeted them with effusive attentions. Outside, the same group that had set off fireworks together on the Fourth of July waited for Grace. Trent slung her bag into the rear of a wagon and handed her up, for Alice had already positioned herself on the bench next to Daniel, who held the reins. Daniel called to the mules, and they were off.

They crossed Young's metal bridge. Soon the road ran by the river, which would have made the journey pleasant had it not been so bumpy. The surface deteriorated more the farther they went from town. Alice dominated the conversation. She spoke of local people and places of which Grace knew nothing.

Grace determined to maintain a pleasant spirit and watched the scenery—rolling, wooded hills and the occasional farm. The occupied acreage consisted for the most part of one-room affairs shingled with cedar or oak, a spring house, a pig or chicken pen, and a barn or shed. Gardens burgeoned with tomatoes, beans, and ripening pumpkins, sometimes staked out with what Amelia told her was a horizontally hung bottle gourd, said to attract purple martins. The martins ate mosquitoes and helped keep crows from the nearby fields, where crops ripened in the summer sun, stalks of corn shooting up in neat rows.

At one house, pausing in stretching threads between two racks, a woman waved to them as they passed. In the break in conversation, Grace asked, "What is she doing?"

Alice gave a laugh. "How do you think these people get their clothes? They don't order them from a seamstress like you do."

Daniel frowned at her. He explained to Grace, "She's using the warping bars to prepare the threads so they can be ready for weaving on the loom. That's what's done with flax or cotton or sheep's wool—after it's combed and carded."

"And spun. See the wheel on the porch?" Amelia pointed. "Some of the women still produce their own dyes from local plants. Pokeweed berries for rose, bloodroot for red, indigo for blue, walnut hulls for brown."

"Oh." Grace had known country people made their own clothing, but she could not imagine so much time being devoted to their creation.

"The original land lots in this area were just over two hundred acres." Daniel spoke over his shoulder and past Alice's pouty face. "The people work hard simply to exist. They learned much from the Cherokees. They burn off sections of their land to plant crops, then after a few years, use the area for grazing, then let it go back to forest while planting new acreage. That system is best on the land. So many of the trees are already being stripped away by the railroads and the copper mines and fed to these new steam-powered sawmills."

Seated across from her, Trent lifted his finger. "But growing produce for the hotels has helped supplement the incomes of some families. Fannie Smith's farm is one of the largest and most profitable."

Daniel nodded. "She's really turned her talent in the kitchen into an industry."

"I hope she has fried chicken for supper," Amelia commented.

"I could stand some now." Trent patted his flat stomach.

Daniel nodded to a clearing by the river. "I can pull over there for us to have a short lunch break."

They all voiced their enthusiasm. Minutes later, they devoured the sandwiches, apples, and cheese Mrs. Wylie had packed into a hamper, the food tasting all the better for their outdoor setting. The mules took a long drink of the river water. When the time came to move on, Grace dragged her feet in getting back into the wagon.

Daniel eyed her. "Would you like to walk with me a while? You and Amelia? You've taken quite a beating in the back."

"I'd love to." Grace ignored Alice's cold stare.

Trent drove the mules with Alice at his side. The rest of them walked ahead to avoid the dust stirred by the wheels. Grace felt much better with some food in her stomach and stretching her aching limbs rather than having to brace herself against the jostling wagon. And of course, it was better with Alice behind them, even glowering as she was, rather than at Daniel's side.

Daniel chuckled. "I've got to tell you a story about Aunt Fannie."

Grace turned an attentive smile on him.

"Tourists used to trade with the Cherokees in these parts. But in the winter, the Indians had it rough. The last of the tribesmen of Chief Gray Eagle would sometimes camp on the Smith property during cold weather. Aunt Fannie would feed them. Many times, she invited them to church. She worked on the chief a long time, and at last, he consented to go with her."

"I've heard this story." Amelia skipped closer to Daniel's side. "Didn't they go to Wolf Creek Baptist?"

"Sure did. When it came time for the sermon, the preacher started off quiet, but then he got going, as Baptists are apt to do." Daniel shot Grace a sideways glance. "He gestured wildly and described the pits of hell. Chief Gray Eagle had never seen a white man carry on like that. He stood up and declared, 'Whiskey too much. Whiskey too much!'"

Everyone laughed, though Grace guessed the others had heard the tale many times. "What happened then?" she asked.

"The chief left, never to return."

"Now if he'd come to an Episcopal church, he surely would have been saved." Amelia giggled.

More laughter. The next instant, Daniel yelled, "Grace!" and lifted her off her feet, drawing her back against him. When she saw the reason, she stumbled and grabbed him.

Trent stopped the mules and backed them up.

"Easy, it's all right," Daniel whispered in her ear, pulling both Grace and Amelia back in a slow retreat from the six-foot-long rattlesnake sunning itself on the road, so motionless it had appeared to be just another stick.

Grace covered her mouth, horrified that she had almost tread on the snake's head. Disturbed by all the commotion, the creature slithered into the grass near the riverbank.

"I—I think I'll ride again," she said.

"I'm sorry...I should've been watching. We see a snake almost every time."

"I'll definitely ride again." Grace clamored into the back of the wagon, not waiting for assistance. As she sat down, she didn't miss the smug smile on Alice's face.

By the time they arrived on the Smith property, Grace was sweaty, sore, and miserable. She surveyed the farm, eager for refreshment. A smaller structure joined the large 1840s cabin by a covered porch. A high board fence just in front of the stacked-stone chimney enclosed a lush garden, where tall green plants clustered thickly together. A woman clad in black came out onto the porch, where several other people already lounged, chatting and sipping lemonade. So they were not Aunt Fannie's only visitors. Grace stifled disappointment and anxiety over the sleeping arrangements.

"Why, it's Rev. Monroe and his town friends," exclaimed the hostess, stepping down with a broad smile. Grace judged her to be about sixty, with her graying dark hair parted in the middle and drawn back into a bun.

Daniel hopped down from the wagon and bounded

over to kiss her hand. "Aunt Fannie, it's been far too long. No one in town can hold up a debate on religion and politics quite like you."

"Oh, nonsense." She swatted him, laughing. "How long are you come for?"

"A night or two, if you've room."

"I've always room."

"And fried chicken?" Amelia inquired as she climbed out of the wagon.

"That, too, Miss Wylie." Fannie Smith turned a welcoming smile on the girl.

"I've brought someone new." Daniel drew Grace forward. The little lady's dark eyes, hooded but sparkling, fell upon her. "Miss Grace Galveston, from New York City."

After Grace curtsied and Fannie bowed her head in acknowledgement, Fannie said, "I had someone from there last week, an architect. Right now there are three from Athens. Students from the university."

The gentlemen on the porch took their cue, rising to meet them. The Thomas brothers, John and Simon, greeted them with great charm and manners, communicated in the warm drawl of Southern gentlemen. The third guest, Richard Carraway, a slender, quiet young man, possessed a passion for botany. His interest provided the group's main reason for their visit to Tallulah, and kept the young man often in the woods.

They took their bags to their rooms. Following Fannie through shadows that persisted inside the cabin even with the shutters open, Grace smiled when Fannie indicated a rope bed covered with a beautiful hand-made quilt that she could share with Amelia. A trundle bed that pulled out below would accommodate Alice. The only other furniture consisted of a trunk at the bed's foot, a cane-back chair, and, to one side of the bed, a little table with an oil lamp perched on a doily.

Long accustomed to having not only her own bed but also her own room, Grace wondered how she would fare sleeping. Unlikely that even the cluster of ribbon-tied lavender Fannie had left on their pillows would help on that score. Grace, however, didn't even let out a sigh with Alice in earshot. They took turns putting away their things and washing the dust away at the basin, using scented lye soap and embroidered hand towels, before venturing into the main part of the house.

With Fannie overseeing the preparation of dinner and Daniel and Trent engaged in a discussion with the university students, the ladies decided to stroll over the property. A man worked in a field among crops laid out in neat rows. Mr. Smith, Grace guessed. As the sun drifted down, igniting a red-orange glow on the horizon, crickets chirped in the thickets. They passed an orchard.

"Apples?" asked Grace.

Amelia nodded. "They do very well here. Settlers used to move around so frequently that they didn't take time to cultivate apple trees. It's really due to the Chero-kees and Jarvis Van Buren—the same one who built in

Clarkesville—that we have the trees around here that we do now."

"What did Mr. Van Buren do?"

"He founded the Georgia Pomological Society in the 1850s and convinced people growing apples would be profitable."

"He also collected mountain varieties and named them," Alice, who trailed along behind them, added.

"Oh, you should taste our own Mountaine Belle!" Amelia rolled her eyes as if she imagined the crunch and the juice on her tongue at that very moment. "There's nothing like a crisp apple on a fall day, with the trees all orange and gold. The farmers have corn shuckings, where all the harvested corn is brought into the barn or a cleared field. Everyone divides into teams to see who can shuck their pile first. Sometimes a red ear is hidden in one pile, and whoever finds it gets a prize. It's all a big party, with lots of food and dancing."

"But, of course, Grace won't be here then, which is just as well, since she'd surely find such an activity quite primitive." Alice raised her chin.

Best to ignore that barb. "It's beautiful here now." Grace sighed. "It's hard to think it could get any prettier."

"Tomorrow we'll take you to Sinking Mountain." Amelia grinned.

"Yes, I've been wondering about that."

Alice edged forward. "After today's travel, the hike might be a bit too much for Miss Galveston. We have to remember, Amelia, she's not accustomed to our terrain."

"Nonsense. It's just a short walk."

"Why is it called 'sinking'?" Grace asked her.

"The ground really is soft. In certain spots, it feels like it's giving way beneath your feet."

"The early settlers decided the Cherokee were right —that the Yunwi Tsundi had a large mining operation under the mountain." Alice pushed her way between them and turned to Grace with feigned concern, the sun glowing on her golden hair. Unfortunately, she really was pretty. "Truly, Miss Galveston, if you need to rest, no one would think the less of you. Some say the view is not very remarkable."

"I'm sure I'll be fine," Grace replied through stiff lips. "It's hardly as if my health is failing."

"The mountain may not look like much at a glance, but the view off the eastern side is wonderful, in *my* opinion," Amelia said. "There's a breathtaking plunge down to the Chattooga River. I believe you'd find it worth the walk."

"It's settled, then." Grace linked her arm through Amelia's, effectively nudging Alice ahead of them.

Amelia gave Grace a conspiratorial smirk.

They returned to the cabin for a meal that justified all the day's hardships. Grace had never tasted more delicious chicken, garden vegetables, and fluffy biscuits with fresh honey. After dinner, one of the students produced a guitar, and they gathered on the porch to enjoy the music floating away into the still night. The ladies helped Aunt Fannie string fresh beans from the garden so that they could be hung to dry, to help feed visitors that would come when the weather was cool and the garden not so verdant. There were no horse hooves, no train whistles, no raucous voices...just perfect tranquility. And Grace loved it.

CHAPTER 8

The following day after breakfast, they took the trail to Sinking Mountain. The students decided to accompany them. Thankfully for Grace, the pace was not vigorous, for the budding botanist kept stopping to exclaim over the flora and fauna and collect samples into a multi-compartmented box. At one point, he pointed and exclaimed with great delight, "Ah, ginseng! See, those plants that look almost like tiny human figures?"

Amelia bent low for a look as Richard pushed back the summer underbrush and decaying leaves. "Yes, it's supposed to have numerous health benefits." She grinned at him. "Rather like a treasure hunt, isn't it?"

Richard returned her smile. "Exactly. This ginseng is not unlike the Chinese variety. It takes years to mature."

"And brings seng hunters a good price at market."

"Aunt Fannie told me that, even years ago, the Cherokee medicine people were said to pass by three stalks before harvesting the fourth."

As Richard squatted and opened his box, Alice huffed. "Apparently, no such compunction has overtaken *you*."

"It's not as though I'm harvesting an immature specimen, *one* specimen," the botany student muttered under his breath.

Walking ahead with her nose in the air, Alice ignored him and Amelia's glare, as well.

The others chuckled to lighten the moment and moved over the next rise. They startled some deer and enjoyed the sight of white tails bobbing as the graceful creatures bounded down the slope. While they waited for Richard to join them again, Daniel told them about the foxes, coyotes, bobcats, and black bears that made their home in the mountains.

Alice remained quiet for the rest of the hike, but Grace could sense her growing irritation as Daniel stayed by Grace's side, sharing interesting facts and offering his hand to help her over fallen trees and jutting roots. When they reached their destination, he sat with Grace looking over the Chattooga River Valley, eating the lunch prepared by Aunt Fannie.

Despite her sweating face and straggling hair, Grace could hardly fail to revel in both the scenery and the company. She did try to keep her laughter muted for Alice's sake. But Daniel's attention made her glow. By the time they again neared the Smith property, the tension from Alice felt almost palpable.

As they sat down to a supper of ham, greens, cornbread, beans, and stewed apples, Alice finally broke her cold silence. "You must find all this quite tedious, Miss Galveston."

"Tedious? Why?" Grace glanced not at Alice, but at Aunt Fannie, who pretended not to notice as she placed a pitcher of sweet tea on the table.

"You're used to such sophisticated amusements in New York."

"I think everyone knows I came here seeking peace, not amusement."

"And why was that? Don't most notable New Yorkers go to Newport for the summer?" Alice narrowed her green eyes.

"Well, yes, but it's hardly a rule."

Everyone chuckled.

"Miss Galveston is an opera singer," Alice told the group from Athens. "Maybe we can coax her to sing for our entertainment tonight."

The men murmured in agreement, but Amelia protested, "Nothing like putting her on the spot."

"Well, Mr. Thomas played his guitar last night. *He* wasn't shy. Surely, if Miss Galveston can sing for the Vanderbilts, our little group wouldn't make her nervous." Alice paused with her fork in midair, pretending to think. "Oh, dear, that's right. Someone said—maybe it was you, Amelia—that some sort of embarrassing incident occurred to prompt this trip? Something about needing to rest your voice, Grace, so you can be ready to return to the stage this fall?"

Alice turned her questioning gaze on Grace, whose face heated. Taken aback at the girl's temerity, she could not find words to reply.

"It wasn't me!" Amelia declared. "I don't know where you heard that."

"Oh. Maybe it was from Daniel, then. I mean, *Rev.* Monroe."

"Hardly." Daniel stiffened in his chair. "Really, Miss Hargrove. I can tell you that Miss Galveston sang most beautifully, and perfectly, while visiting with us at my parents' home."

Grace smiled at him while Alice's mouth firmed at the reminder—and the rebuke.

John Thomas, the most outgoing and gallant of the students, responded to the awkwardness of the situation by chiming in, "Actually, instead of making you all listen to my inexpert strumming again, I was hoping Miss Wylie would join me for a game of checkers tonight."

Amelia looked up with her jaw slack. "Me?"

"I do love a good game of checkers, and I hear the same of you."

"Oh, yes—I'd love to!" She didn't seem to notice Richard Carraway's suddenly downcast expression.

As they rose from dinner, Daniel volunteered to assist Aunt Fannie in clearing the table. She took him up on his offer but shooed away all other attempts to help. Alice watched Grace. Grace had expected Alice to retreat in the face of her companions' disapproval. Instead, the girl's growing resentment would apparently not let her rest...or Grace either.

"It's because he'll talk politics with her," Alice said as they left the table. "Aunt Fannie always campaigns all over the county for her candidates and has her family do the same. Daniel will be a while. What will you do?"

"I'm sure I'll find something." Grace started to move away, but where could she go to escape the girl?

"You must feel like a fish out of water, being out here in the absolute wilderness." False sympathy filled Alice's tone. "In town during the tourist season, that's one thing. But when the people leave, even Tallulah is quite a small-town. Almost as quiet as it is, well, right now. You must be looking forward to returning to New York."

"Not really."

"But surely, you'll have to go back and take up your singing soon. I'm sure once you get swept up in all the glamour of that scene, this will seem like a dream." She gave a careless laugh. "As though you've never even been here."

"You'd like that, wouldn't you, Alice?" Grace snapped, her patience gone at last. Not waiting for a reaction, she turned on her heel and marched across the room and onto the front porch, where Mr. Thomas and Amelia set up for their game. Mr. Carraway perched on the top step and scratched with a fountain pen in a small notebook. They all looked up as she stomped past.

"Where are you going?" Amelia asked.

"For a walk. I need some fresh air." Grace tossed her reply over her shoulder.

"Do you want me to go with you?" Faintly. Not enthusiastic.

"No, that's all right."

"Well, it's almost dark. Don't be gone long."

"I won't go far."

But as she walked, it felt good, and she found herself on the trail to Sinking Mountain that they had taken earlier in the day. She could hardly get lost going that way.

Why had she let Alice's silly comments stir her up so? Maybe because while the girl's tactics were childish, her words did contain some truth. Grace soon would have to return to New York. The thought made her feel empty. She wanted to sing, she *did*. But not to gain her father's admiration. She would just have to settle it in her mind once and for all that Hampton Galveston's opinion had no bearing on her career.

She sighed, for not caring about what her father thought would be just as impossible as not wanting to see the affection in Daniel Monroe's eyes. And what could come of that? They could write, of course, and she could vacation here again next summer. But what might happen between now and then, over the course of a whole year? She would have to answer Blake Greene's expected question of matrimony, and Daniel might notice what a gem had always been right here beneath his nose...Amelia.

As a whip-o-will sounded a mournful note, Grace stopped. She had been so involved in her inner ramblings that she had failed to notice the sun dropping below the horizon. The soft curve of the hills now offered only a darkening silhouette. She better go back.

Retracing her steps, she had not gone far when she came to a fork in the path that she hadn't noticed passing earlier. Well, it had to be the one that led downhill, not the trail continuing around the mountain. She must have gone farther and faster than she had intended.

After walking several more minutes without the Smith farm coming into view, Grace's heart began to beat fast, faster than the exertion of her exercise called for. She could *not* have gotten lost on such a short walk.

Shadows deepened among the lush underbrush. There was nothing to do but continue. After a few minutes, though, the path began to wind upward. That was all wrong. Grace stopped and wrung her hands. Maybe if she were closer to the homestead than she thought, they would hear if she called out.

"Hello? Hello!"

Her voice rang back at her. Then the silence mocked.

Maybe she should go back the other way. As she

turned and strode ahead, her boot caught on an exposed root, sending her flying over the edge of the hillside. She grabbed for a sapling, but her momentum kept her going. She screamed as she tumbled headlong into a dense stand of mountain laurel. It closed around her like an evil curtain. She was sliding, sliding. The limbs plucked at her clothing and scraped her skin, and she covered her head to protect her face.

Then, she lay motionless at last. Grace tried to push the branches away, but any attempt to move, to ascertain the way out, brought pain from the many claw-like thorns grasping her. Hadn't Daniel told them about "laurel hells," places where the plants grew so thick they choked out all other growth and even the light? Hunting dogs and even sometimes people who became entangled had been known to never emerge. And now she was in the midst of one.

Grace fought back panic. They would come looking for her. She just had to remain calm and try to get out into the opening. Keeping her face down as much as possible, she crawled slowly forward. Tears filled her eyes as thorns tore through her light-weight blouse and into her skin. A sob escaped her, and she was about to lie down in hopelessness when she noticed a lightening to her left. Grace edged her painstaking way in that direction.

Seemingly an eternity later, she broke free!

The ground leveled out for a space before dropping again into a dark ravine. She huddled next to a tree on the flat surface. She had no idea which way to go. She simply must wait and hope the men would find her soon. Besides, she had twisted her ankle when she fell, and it ached now. She rubbed it, gaze darting around.

Something rustled on the forest floor. With a shudder, she thought of the rattler they had seen the day before. If one crept up on her, it was too dark now for her to know until it was too late. Never had she been so helpless. It seemed an appropriate time to do something unusual. Pray.

Grace's attempts to wing her requests heavenward were cut short by a sound that turned her blood cold and raised the tiny hairs on the back of her neck. A sound she had never heard before. A cry of the utmost suffering, like a woman's dying scream. A bobcat. And not too far away. The last bit of her composure gone, she covered her head with her arms, crying and trembling.

CHAPTER 9

*D*aniel dried dishes with a checked towel, giving Mrs. Smith his reflections on the performance of the current Tallulah Falls commissioners, when Amelia walked into the kitchen.

"You're still here?" she asked.

"Well, yes, there were a lot of dishes." He flashed her a smile, but her worried expression caused him to add, "Why? Is something wrong?"

"If Grace isn't with you, something's *very* wrong."

Aunt Fannie turned from the sink to look at Amelia, and Daniel put down his cloth. He stepped toward her. "Tell me."

"She went out for a walk after dinner. Alice kept nettling her. I assumed she had returned by now. But I —didn't check." Tears filled her eyes. "I was too involved in my game."

"Tell the men," Fannie directed Amelia. "I'll fetch lanterns and guns."

As she hurried out, Daniel's gaze met Amelia's. They didn't need to say that Grace should have returned long ago...that anything could have happened. Daniel asked, "Which way did she go?"

Amelia shook her head. "I don't know. I'm sorry."

They began by combing the farm, yelling "Grace!" When no reply resulted, Daniel debated between taking the rutted road into town or the smooth and pleasant trail toward Sinking Mountain. While the other men hiked off down the road, he and Trent took the trail, splitting up at the fork.

Daniel had not gone far after turning left when the cry of a bobcat froze him in his tracks. He carried a loaded gun, and he was a good shot. He hurried on, anxious to get to Grace, imagining her lost and maybe hurt. The forest could be terrifying at night to a woman accustomed only to city life. He paused, lifted the lantern, and yelled, "Grace!"

No response. He continued, calling her name at regular intervals. Maybe the cat would slink away toward the river, discouraged by all the commotion. Bobcats generally proved non-aggressive unless provoked.

Then, at last—a voice!

"I'm here! Daniel, down here!"

Downhill from where he stood on the path, a form crumpled against a tree, not far from the edge of a sea of laurel and rhododendron. Grace! She rose, leaning on the tree trunk for support.

"Are you all right?" he called.

"Scratched—I fell into the laurel—and terrified—"

Daniel slid down the hill on the flats of his boots, the gun in one hand and the lantern in the other. Placing both at her feet, he leaned in, cradled her face in his hands, and kissed her. Not gently. Intensely.

Her arms went around him, and her soft lips parted beneath his. He didn't have to think, didn't *want* to think, because it was the very thing they had both been wanting to happen. Giving in to relief and emotion, Daniel held nothing back. He had never kissed a woman like this.

Grace trembled in his arms and, turning her face downward, sagged against him as if her strength were spent. He dropped his arms to her waist, holding her up.

"Should I apologize?" he whispered.

"If you do, I'll never forgive you. Thank you for coming for me."

But the dim light revealed scratches on her face. He touched one and his finger came away wet. "You're bleeding."

"The laurel. I was so afraid I'd never get out of it."

"And your clothes are torn." With horror, he took in the ripped white fabric, already darkened with blood. He shrugged out of his vest and carefully slipped her arms through the holes. "I'm sorry. What a cad I was to not even notice, to just grab you like that."

"No." Grace touched his face. "I'm so glad—so glad you came."

Her voice choked on a sob, and he kissed her again. She stepped in close, shivering, seeming to need his nearness. Her body fit so neatly against his. He had only ever imagined such magic. He wanted to love and protect this woman forever. Then guilt overcame passion, and he drew back, saying, "We should get you back, let Aunt Fannie look at those cuts."

"*Scratches.*"

"Yeah, right. Let's go."

Grace took a few steps and stopped. She shook her head as Daniel gave her a questioning look. "I'm afraid it's going to take me a while, and I'm going to need your arm to lean on. My ankle—it twisted when I fell. It's not bad. I can walk, if you'll be patient with me."

"Nonsense." Daniel slung the strap of the gun across his back and handed Grace the glowing lantern. Then, despite her gasp of surprise, he placed one arm under her back and a hand under her knees, and picked her up.

"I'm sorry," he said as she winced in pain. As careful as he could be, he headed up the hill, back to the path.

"Daniel, this is very gallant, but you're a preacher, not a lumberjack. No one would expect you to carry me all the way back."

"I can do it. You're light as a feather."

"Say that again in five minutes."

He puffed a laugh. "So long as I don't have to carry on a conversation, I can do it," he repeated.

With that, Grace laid her head against his shoulder and went as still as a little girl. He did feel rather like a conquering knight. When they met up with Trent, he refused assistance even though he was growing winded. He carried Grace into the cabin, ignoring Alice's wide-eyed stare and Amelia's clamoring.

Once he deposited Grace on the bed, Fannie set to work washing the blood from her face. Daniel told her of the hurt ankle.

"Elevate it, and I'll prepare a poultice."

She called for her granddaughter to help her make a healing salve for the scratches. The girl went into the garden after aloe while Fannie unwrapped herbs from paper packets.

Amelia sat beside Grace and started to unlace her boots, saying, "Grace, I'm so sorry. I should have gone with you. It's all my fault."

"It certainly was not. And really, I can unlace my own boot."

They both stopped and looked at Daniel hovering in the corner of the room. "You'll have to go," they said in unison, which would have caused him to laugh had he been less concerned.

Fannie turned from her work to behold Daniel's slack stare. "She'll be fine," the woman urged. "But I have to tend those cuts. You've done your part. Now go."

Daniel remembered the torn bodice under his vest Grace wore and rose. "I'll be back later," he assured Grace.

"You'll see her in the morning," Fannie told him, gentle but firm.

"But Mrs. Smith—"

"In the morning."

Recognizing defeat, Daniel decided to retreat. But not before he bent and, in front of watching eyes, placed a gentle kiss on Grace's forehead.

"Thank you," she murmured again.

As he closed the door behind him, Fannie said, "My, but our reverend is a goner."

~

The next day, irritation gnawed at Daniel's insides. Trent would be willing to drive the wagon, allowing him to ride in the back with Grace, who perched in as comfortable a position as possible with her foot up on a valise. No doubt, his advances last night made her want—even expect—that. But he chose to drive. At least maybe his silence would finally give Alice the message that she did not interest him.

Women had always swooned over his appearance. But his mother had taught him that true beauty came from within, so he should handle feminine attentions with both courtesy and modesty. For the truly determined, he administered the perfect test by disclosing his occupation. That weeded them out pretty quickly.

Grace, however, seemed drawn to him on all levels, not at all discouraged by his strong spiritual foundation. In fact, she responded well to his Christian qualities. But was that because she shared them, or she needed them?

He frowned. He had let himself drift along, satisfied by surface comments, drawn into a relationship without having a clear sense of her faith when differences between them in this area could prove a far greater obstacle than mere geography.

He felt her studying him, sensed her wondering at this change in his demeanor. He turned and smiled his assurance, the sight of her wide brown eyes melting him to his core. "Doing all right?" he asked. "Need a break?"

"I'm fine."

Daniel returned to his reverie, rubbing his two-day growth of beard with one hand. He must look a sight. Not only did he need a shave and a good bath, but his eyes were probably bloodshot too. He had not slept well last night. The thoughts that flooded his mind while kissing her kept repeating themselves like some sort of romantic mantra—*to love and protect*. The phrase came straight from the vows of holy matrimony! Was he really in love with Grace Galveston? They must have a talk, and soon.

He spent the rest of the journey in silent and intent

conversation with God about this woman who was driving him crazy.

They pulled up in front of the hotel. Daniel jumped down and walked around to the rear of the wagon, just as Amelia helped Grace swing her legs down. He managed a crooked smile. "Shall I carry you in, ma'am?"

"Let's not make a scene." Grace looked around at the throngs of people, far more than were usual even for the summer. Until that moment, Daniel had forgotten about the aerialist.

"I think if we both take an arm, she can manage," Amelia suggested.

Daniel grabbed Grace's valise and assisted as instructed. In this manner, they helped her into the lobby.

"What in the world...?" Martha Hampton strode toward them, gaping at her niece.

Salve still shone on the scratches on Grace's fair skin. She wore the untorn dress she had packed. But while it at least covered the cuts on her torso, today's travel left the material stained and winkled.

"This is the last time you go off into the wilderness, the *last time!*" Martha shook her finger at Grace as though she were a wayward five-year-old.

"I'm fine, Aunt Martha. Mrs. Smith said you won't even be able to see the scratches in a few days, and my ankle was merely twisted, not sprained. I can walk just fine." And she shook off her assistants to demonstrate that fact.

An explanation was in order. Daniel cleared his throat. "Miss Galveston went for a walk alone yesterday and fell down a slope into some laurel."

Grace shrugged. "What's a wilderness adventure without getting lost at least once?"

Her attempt at lightheartedness failed in light of that one revealing word.

"*Lost*? Oh, good heavens! What were you people doing, letting her go off alone?" Martha flung her hand out. "Look at you. This is *not* what I had in mind for your reunion. What will Blake Greene think? I knew I sacrificed my better judgment by letting you go off to this Fannie Mae's—"

"Fannie Smith's," corrected Amelia.

But Daniel watched Grace, who turned pale and repeated, "Blake Greene?"

"Yes, Blake Greene." Martha huffed.

"He's here?"

"Yes, it was to be a surprise. I made his reservation when I made ours, after he told me that he would be able to take a break from his firm later in the summer."

Amelia looked between Grace and her aunt. "What does this Blake Greene person have to do with anything?" She posed the question stuck in Daniel's throat.

Martha turned to her, brows raised. "A great deal, once he finally speaks his mind—which I have no doubt he has come to do." She turned her sharp, withering gaze on Daniel.

A thousand Chinese firecrackers snapped and fizzled inside his head. Grace's lips trembled. And he had thought her so honest, so open! "Why didn't you tell me you had a fiancé?" His voice came out like a growl.

Grace lifted her hands. "He's not my fiancé!"

But the undisguised distress on her face showed he was *something*.

At that moment, a disbelieving masculine voice spoke from the stairs. "Grace?"

A tall young man stood on the steps. A top hat, linen frock coat suit, and silk cravat provided tailored presentation for the man's wheat-blond hair, blue eyes, aristocratically proportioned features, and muscular frame. The picture of modern power and wealth. His expression betrayed both joy and concern as it fastened on the object of his affection. Then he jogged down to meet her, bracing his hands on her arms and kissing her forehead.

"What has happened to you, my dear?"

Grace drew back, obviously flustered. "I—Blake, this is Amelia Wylie, my friend, and—"

Mr. Greene made a chivalrous bow over Amelia's hand, then turned toward Daniel. The man's hand came out. Daniel's hand, like his face, felt frozen. Not for all the good breeding in the world could make it leave his side.

Martha Hampton gazed on him with a smug smirk.

But Blake Greene could not be faulted for his almost-fiancée's two-timing. Daniel forced himself to shake hands just as Mr. Greene started to give up and lower his.

"Rev. Daniel Monroe, Grace's other *friend*," Daniel said. His voice sounded cold. He glanced at Grace, whose expression pled for understanding. For a chance to explain. Daniel couldn't give it. "Clearly, Miss Galveston is back in good hands, so I'll be taking my leave."

He didn't wait for anyone else to speak but spun on his heel and marched away. Grace called to him in an anguished tone. He let the door swing shut behind him.

CHAPTER 10

*T*wo days later, Grace's desperation to talk with Daniel escalated to such an intensity that she felt only impatience with the commotion surrounding the feat scheduled for the aerialist J. A. St. John, son of the 1884 Prohibition Party presidential candidate. The impossible crowds made locating the young minister all the less likely. Trains backed up for over a mile, bringing spectators from as far away as South Carolina, Florida, and Alabama. Publicists billed the Tallulah Gorge walk as the highest and longest ever to be attempted. St. John would balance himself with a forty-six pound, thirty-foot-long pole as he crossed 1,440 feet across the chasm—with a drop of around a thousand feet to the rushing waters below.

Gracious and patient with Grace's fretting, Amelia agreed to go a second time to Daniel's home and also to the church. On this occasion, she took a note to stick under the door should she find him again absent.

Daniel, please, we need to talk. If you are unable to come before, I will attend the ball tonight at the hotel. Grace Galveston.

"This is so not like him," Amelia told Grace when she joined her for tea at The Cliff House, having delivered the note to the residence but seen no trace of the occupant. "He's usually so calm and level-headed."

"Do you think he'll come tonight?"

Amelia shrugged, then said, "Doubtful. Daniel has nothing against dancing, but some of his older parishioners do, so he doesn't frequent the ballroom scene." She glanced up from stirring cream into her brew just as Grace's face crumpled. "But who knows. He has to face you sooner or later."

"Does he?"

"Unless he's totally taken leave of his senses, his personality will urge him to have things out in the open and settled. He's not the type to let people dangle. Perhaps he just needs to think through some things." Amelia took a sip of her tea. She put down the cup, fidgeted, cleared her throat. "Grace, you and I have not spoken much of spiritual matters. I wish now that we had. I'm not sure exactly where you stand, but I do know that any woman who might become Daniel's wife would—"

She stopped, looking over Grace's shoulder. When her brow furrowed, Grace twisted to find Blake Greene approaching.

"Odds are running even to two-to-one that Leon won't complete the walk," he said as he pulled out a chair and sat down.

"*Won't* complete it?" Amelia frowned. "Surely, they don't think...?"

Blake lifted a shoulder. He leaned back and crossed one leg over the other, popping a lemon tart into his mouth.

"You didn't bet, did you?" Grace angled away from the swirl of his strong cologne.

Blake grinned. "My dear, with odds like that, what man could resist?"

Daniel would resist.

"I laid a neat bundle in *favor* of the daring gent. There's quite a scene out there...vendors selling food and drink...that Mr. Young selling souvenir photos of Leon...more people arriving by the minute. Folks estimate more than six thousand may come today. I'd suggest if you ladies are almost finished with tea, we might wish to secure our spots along the rim."

Grace glanced toward the stairs. "We have to wait on Aunt Martha. She was still napping when we came down."

Blake frowned. "Should you go up and check on her? Someone could move the stools we set out this morning. Unfortunately, not everyone in attendance will share our code of conduct."

Grace sighed and rose to do as he suggested. Before turning away, she patted Amelia's arm. "We'll talk later," she promised.

Amelia offered a faint smile. "All right. I must go meet my parents now, anyway."

When she and Amelia left the table, Blake sat back down to finish up the leftovers. He could hardly be termed doting. But at the same time, he seemed quite confident of his claim on her. After Grace's initial vague explanation that Daniel was a new friend with whom she'd had a misunderstanding, Blake seemed to wave off the incident in the lobby. He'd laughingly referred a few times since to "that mad minister." He didn't seem to notice how that made Grace bristle.

Half an hour later, on Blake's arm, Grace made her way through the throngs. Martha sailed along at Blake's other side. In view of his height and imposing appearance, most people fell away in front of them. Ladies stared at him as much as men did at Grace. They made a smart couple, well able to hold their own even strolling down Fifth Avenue. But she shrank from the attention. Her gait was quite normal and her scratches were almost healed, easily covered with a bit of facial powder, thanks to the medications Aunt Fannie had sent back with her. So maybe her reticence came more from the fact that so many people had recently seen her on Daniel's arm...or worse, that *he* might be anywhere in the crowd, watching her.

Grace took a seat on the stool they had brought and raised her parasol. She fixed her gaze on the spider web of guy wires supporting the main rope Leon would traverse. But her mind lingered on her personal dilemma.

Daniel had never spoken of love or marriage. Yet his actions—and his kiss—had told her much. And if he didn't care, why had he stormed off at the sight of Blake? If he were at the ball tonight, she would find a few private moments in which to explain that yes, Blake had been courting her in New York, but that she hadn't mentioned it because she had hardly thought of him since meeting Daniel.

That would provide the perfect opening for them to discuss their feelings for one another. And if it came to that, what then? Like a tightrope walker, would she be willing to put everything on the line, do whatever she must, to have his love?

The crowd exploded into excited talk and cheering. At the far side of the gorge, a slender man with curling dark hair and moustache, wearing a body-fitting costume, approached Inspiration Point.

"There he is," Blake said, though even a simpleton couldn't mistake the identity of the man carrying the huge pole.

Martha announced, "This is the craziest thing I have ever seen."

At 5:20, Professor Leon stepped onto the rope and slowly, methodically, started forward. Grace scanned the faces of spectators jammed into every nook and cranny and lining the balconies of the nearby hotels. All portrayed anxiety and fear, watching in tense silence.

Grace held her breath as she tracked the progress of the small, vulnerable figure, balancing above the maw of the earth. How must the man's poor wife and four-year-old daughter feel, watching not far away? How must they feel *every* time Mr. St. John took such a risk? Surely, the suspense must wear on them.

Suddenly, a loud snapping noise shot through the air. A collective gasp issued forth as the main line, upon which the professor stood not yet halfway over the gorge, began to sway dramatically. Grace rose, hand at her heart. People cried out. Leon made several exaggerated movements to maintain his balance. Grace pictured him plunging to the floor of the canyon, his spirit flying to meet his Maker. She couldn't breathe. Her corset was so tight! The aerialist took several steps forward, dropped to one knee, and sat on the rope.

One of Leon's assistants raced to fix the dangling support line. Then, a cry of alarm came up from the gorge and spread like wildfire through the nervous crowd. The line had been cut!

"Who would do such a thing?" Grace gasped.

Blake looked grave. "Perhaps one of those who bet against the professor."

"*That's* why I don't like gambling. Greed could cause that man to die!" She jabbed her fan toward the figure still sitting on the wire.

Blake had the good sense to remain silent. Men filed down into the gorge to serve as lookouts for the other ropes, while the damaged one was retied. Grace imagined herself in the professor's position. Would *she* be ready to meet her Maker? A deep shiver coursed through her, and a tiny flicker of realization lit inside her head. Daniel wasn't the only one with much to settle.

How she needed him. The fact that he had answers to life's deepest questions, and her deepest needs, made him stabilizing as well as fascinating. And she would do anything—give up her career, her dreams of singing *Aïda* to adoring fans, the promise of wealth and acclaim —to be by Daniel's side. He completed her. *He* was a sure bet.

A heavy weight lifted from her chest and drifted into the blue sky. She sank down onto her stool, light-headed.

"He's moving!"

Professor Leon rose ever so slowly to his feet. As he began to inch toward them again, he scowled, muttering to himself. Finally, finally, he stepped onto Lover's Leap. The whole thing took less than a half hour. Her husband's safety guaranteed, Mrs. St. John collapsed in a heap of bustled skirts and petticoats. Grace could barely see what was happening around all the clamoring people. Word spread that the woman was revived and Leon's personal physician and crowd members argued against the aerialist making the contracted return trip. To his credit, Mr. Young agreed with them. The family was trundled off to their rooms at The Grand View, and Grace sought hers at The Cliff House.

With so much on the line, she craved time to prepare for her next meeting with Daniel.

~

A building sense of excitement and confidence left Grace unable to nap. Instead, she laid on the now-familiar bed and imagined different scenarios and how she would respond, what she would say. For the more she pondered it, the more sure she became that a man with Daniel Monroe's sense of honor would not ignore a lady's direct plea for a conference. His inbred consideration would prevent him from leaving her in an indefinite state of distress.

She must be beautiful. Grace didn't have to think long on what to wear. The evening dress of gold silk with *Watkins, New York* on the label cried out for redemption. She had failed in it before, but it was a gown meant for triumphant moments. This time would be different.

When she was ready, Grace knocked softly on her aunt's door. A voice called for her to enter.

Aunt Martha reclined on her chaise lounge, a damp cloth draping her forehead. "Good, I'm glad I didn't have to press you to join the party tonight," she said. "Mr. Greene grows impatient with your 'headaches'... although I seem to be having one myself now."

"Yes, he asked me to meet him at eight." She didn't add that she had ordered a supper tray to her room to avoid the possibility of having to take that meal alone with Blake.

"I hope you've tired of your games and put that preacher out of your mind. It's time to stop thinking about summer romances."

"Why would you oppose a match between myself and Rev. Monroe?" Grace mentally girded herself for battle.

Her aunt chortled. "A match? Ha!"

"Why not? You saw yourself the type of family from which he comes."

Aunt Martha surveyed her with more careful consideration, as if weighing Grace's gravity. "For a local girl, yes, he could be considered a catch. His family has money and charm. Even old money. But you need to think of your future, all you've worked for. Would you throw all that away to be some backwoods preacher's wife? To live on his salary? Never to sing in public again? And maybe even to follow him to God-knows-what forsaken place to preach to the heathen?"

"Yes."

The word, calm but undoubtedly firm, fell like a

weight in the room. Aunt Martha stared at her for a minute, then closed her eyes, raised her brows, and drew in a deep breath as though to retreat from the reality just spoken. She waved a hand in Grace's direction. "I can't deal with you just now, Grace. Not when you're making no sense like this." But the next second, Aunt Martha's eyes popped open and her voice sharpened. "But you'd better be prepared to give Mr. Greene the answer he deserves. Don't you dare reject him after the way you've strung him along."

"I'm sorry if I've encouraged Blake to no end," Grace replied in a softer tone. "But I never felt for him what I do for Daniel. I knew something was missing...I just didn't know what. Now I know what it feels like to love someone so much you can hardly breathe."

"Balderdash! Sentimental mumbo-jumbo! Security is what lasts. A woman must make her own accomplishments so she is never helpless. A woman must have money, money of her own. Everything else is unreliable."

Grace's brow puckered as she heard her aunt's vulnerability speaking. She dropped to a sitting position on the edge of the settee. "Are you saying that because you care about me—because you don't want to see what happened to my mother happen to me? Because of what happened to *you*?"

"Of course. I'd never wish that on you."

"Daniel is not like my father, Aunt. He would never abandon the people for whom he is responsible. I think..." She paused, reflecting, then hurried on. "I think you're saying these things because being around Daniel's family made you remember all you lost. I'm sorry for that, Aunt Martha, but I have to make my own decisions and plan for my own future. The vision of success and money in New York was never truly mine. And my heart tells me that even if I never sang another note, but I was with Daniel, I would be happy."

Aunt Martha's eyes filled with tears. The clock ticked on the bedside table. Then, her aunt leaned forward, and in a rare gesture of tenderness, placed her hand on Grace's hair. "You are so like your mother," she whispered with emphasis. "Don't make her same mistakes."

"The men with whom we fell in love are vastly different. It will be all right, Aunt Martha." Grace kissed the wrinkled fingers and rose, her skirts rustling.

With a full heart, she descended to the ballroom.

Blake Greene waited for her in the lobby. His eyes lit, and he gave her a smile that would thaw any woman's heart. She did care for him. He had infused affection into her cold world. He was fun, dashing, and generous. She would have to explain things to him, but not tonight. If she could just maneuver things so that she had time alone with Daniel first...

As they entered the ballroom, the dancers performed a lively polka-redowa. Grace managed to get a good look around the room as they went for some punch, thus ascertaining Daniel was not there yet. She suggested they take some seats near the entrance from where they could enjoy the music of the brass band and view the dancing. Blake acquiesced, but he soon grew impatient. He was the type to be on the center of the floor with a beautiful woman in his arms, not stuck on the sidelines. At last, she could put him off no longer.

The music called for a hesitation waltz, a variation of the Boston. Grace and Blake had danced it together before in New York. The dramatic pauses, exaggerated leg movements and backbends showcased Blake's style. As they danced, Grace's train swept up on her arm, the gas lights causing her gown to shimmer like liquid gold, people gathered to watch. Only a few other couples on the periphery attempted a less vigorous form of the waltz.

"I'm glad I came," Blake told her. "I missed you."

How to reply with both kindness and truth?

He saved her from answering by continuing. "You're lovely. I haven't been as expressive as I should have been this past year, but I hope my presence here speaks clearly of my feelings for you."

"Yes. I—was definitely surprised. I know what it meant for you to leave your firm and travel all the way to Georgia."

"Do you?" He swept her back over his arm, one brow raised, watching her intently.

This conversation barreled fast in the wrong direction—and in the middle of the dance floor! Had he already spoken with her father? Grace had a terrifying vision of Blake getting down on one knee and presenting her with a ring right there with everyone watching.

Then, when a black-clad figure tapped Blake's shoulder, relief like that of the curtain closing on a successful performance swept her. Her eyes widened. Daniel stood there, the picture of an aristocrat, dark hair slicked back from his forehead, one hand behind his waist and the other tucked into a white silk embroidered vest.

Before he had a chance to speak, Blake voiced his displeasure in a single syllable. "*You?*"

Daniel bowed. "I'm sorry to interrupt, but I believe I have business with Miss Galveston."

"Couldn't it wait until after this dance?" Blake asked tersely.

"It's pressing business." A muscle in Daniel's jaw twitched. "Besides, considering the ankle injury this lady recently suffered, I fear for her health."

Grace bit back a laugh.

The insinuation of carelessness made Blake's face red and his posture rigid. "I would hardly have asked her to dance had I not *known* her ankle is healed... having been in her constant company these past couple of days."

"Really, gentlemen." Grace tapped Blake with her fan to try to separate the two. They looked like bantam roosters ready to spar, making her battle the urge to giggle. "There's no need to make such a fuss. Mr.

Greene, I'm sure it will only require a short interlude for Mr. Monroe to dispense with his 'pressing business.' Perhaps we can dance again after that."

Blake settled a formal mask over a seething interior, obviously incensed at this dismissal just when his passions had warmed toward a declaration of his intentions. But being a gentleman, he could hardly argue with a lady. He backed away. Doubtless, he expected Daniel to escort her off the floor, just as she did. But as she turned in preparation to take Daniel's arm, Daniel drew her to him in a firm waltz position. Their eyes met, hers wide.

"The music continues," he said softly. "If you'll dance with me, I promise not to mop the floor with you like that—"

"Daniel," she scolded.

"Just dance with me."

"I thought you didn't dance."

"Who told you that?"

As they began to waltz, several gasps illustrated her statement. She did giggle then. "It seems Amelia was right. She told me some of your older parishioners preferred a minister who avoided the dance floor."

"Just this one time, I'm willing to risk their censure. Who can blame a man for losing his senses over you? That's exactly what I did, not just tonight when I saw you dancing with Greene, but the first time I met you."

Grace remained silent, awed that Daniel spoke to her in the very manner of which she had dreamed. He held her close, his voice soft in her ear. He took unfaltering, yet smaller steps, allowing for the weakened ankle. Thoughtful, protective, as always.

He continued. "I'm afraid I've developed a pattern of acting irrationally around you, Miss Galveston. It was stupid of me to storm out as I did earlier this week."

"You were taken by surprise."

"There is no excuse for my behavior. I acted—not like a gentleman, nor certainly as a Christian—but like a child."

Meeting his eyes, she shook her head. "No. You didn't. Please, it is I who have much to explain—much to tell you."

At last, the music ended. Daniel bowed, and she curtsied. They had finished the dance across the room from where Blake had retreated, near an exit. Daniel gestured toward it. "Then I suggest we take a stroll, for I need to talk with you, too, Grace."

CHAPTER 11

$\mathcal{D}$aniel led Grace past the crowds of people in ball finery on the porch, out onto the lawn. Water spilling from a tiered fountain splashed silver in the moonlight. Here a quiet enveloped them, tantalizing and romantic. But he could no longer be led by his feelings. He'd allowed things to come too far, too fast. He knew all too well the biblical commandment for believers to avoid yoking with nonbelievers. But even though two days of spiritual searching undergirded his determination to be honest, dread sat in his stomach like a boulder.

He debated with himself how he should open this conversation when Grace spoke. "I should have told you about Blake. It's true, he called on me frequently in New York. Aunt Martha strongly favors a match. Until this summer, I went along with the idea, not because I really desired it, but because it seemed my most reasonable option."

"It's all right." Daniel patted her arm. "As I said, I overreacted. It would be stupid of me to think you didn't have many admirers back home. Besides, it's not as though any declarations have been made between us."

She stopped walking and searched his eyes. "But... much has passed between us, nonetheless."

"It has," he agreed in a grave tone. "And at my initiation. I'm usually much more...cautious. But what I said inside was true. For the first time where a woman was concerned, I've found myself acting first and thinking later. These past two days, I've realized that—there is much we don't know about one another."

Grace nodded, touching the tip of her fan to her chin, a frown flittering over her face. "I realize we have led very different lives."

He sat on a wrought iron bench and patted the seat beside him. Grace obliged. Thus shielded from public view by the waxy leaves of a huge magnolia tree, Daniel turned to her. "Yes, we have. And I wonder if you realize just how simple mine is, centered on home, family, and most importantly, my faith in Christ."

"Well, of course. You're a minister. Those things *must* be important to you."

"But you see, that's just it. It's not as though I were a lawyer whose clients were important or a teacher whose students were important just because it's all wrapped up in my occupation, my livelihood. Not that those people may not care about their clients and students, but—what I'm trying to say is, my faith is not important to me because I'm a minister. My ministry is important to me because my faith is the core of who I am. It effects *everything* about my life. Sharing the love of God and His power of salvation with people is the central purpose of each day."

Grace gave a slight smile. "Well, I don't suppose it matters which comes first, the chicken or the egg. What matters is the result—that you are who you are, and that's what I appreciate about you."

Daniel groaned inwardly. *Lord, help me. Let me get on Your path and not get off.* He took her hand in his, looked deep into her brown eyes. Annoying how the soft kid of her long gloves kept him from touching her skin. In a vague way, it symbolized a much deeper barrier rising between them. *Cut to the chase.* "Anyone who shares my life must have the same focus."

She swallowed, clearly responding to the seriousness of his implication. "Today, I realized something." She spoke slowly, softly. "Money, acclaim, comforts—they are all empty when you possess them but are alone. I would give them all up in a second if it meant..." She stopped, drew a breath, and started again. "You talk of your life being simple. Maybe the simple things are best. I don't mind your focus on your ministry. It's admirable. I think...you probably have enough love for everyone and enough faith for both of us." She gave a light laugh, but it came out throaty.

But Daniel remained silent. He stared at his hands holding hers. *Oh, God, I did run ahead of You. But why, oh, why, did I—do I—feel these things for her, if it's not meant to be?*

"Please, say something."

"Whatever I say is going to be inadequate." Seconds ticked by. Her expression began to change from expectation to uncertainty. This beautiful woman had just laid her heart on the line. He was a mess inside, joy and sorrow battling because of her admission. His natural response, what he *wanted* to do, would be to take her in his arms and whisper words of love and commitment. But the part of him attuned to spiritual prompting urged caution. Stalling for time, he murmured, "I'm... deeply humbled that you feel that way."

"I don't want you to be humbled." Grace's brows drew together, and a trace of vulnerability trembled in her tone. "I want you to be happy!"

"I am—I certainly never thought to be hearing such words from you—and I know what they cost you. I know what it would mean, what you'd be giving up, to open your heart to me. But I'm also afraid."

"Afraid? Of what?"

"That if we don't share the same priorities, our feelings may not be enough." He studied her, waiting.

"But I just told you..." Grace withdrew her hands, her back stiffening.

"Yes, about the money and the fame. I've always known you weren't that sort of person."

"Then what? I go to church every Sunday, I try to obey the commandments and live an upstanding life. It's hardly as though I'm some heathen."

"I know that. Grace, it was your gentleness, your openness—your inward as well as outward beauty that drew me. But there is more to it than that. In Ephesians, it makes it clear—'by grace are ye saved through faith; and that not of yourselves: it is the gift of God: not of works...' Even if we do good relying on our own power, we fail. It's impossible for our motivations to always be pure. It's impossible for us to do enough to save ourselves. The Bible tells us there is no one righteous. If we think we don't need God, we sin by that very attitude."

"Are you saying I'm a sinner?"

"No worse a sinner than every person, myself included. Even having submitted my life and will to God—because I know that He alone knows what is truly best for me—I fail daily. But I know the grace He extended when He died for all of us on the cross covers all my sins and weaknesses, when I ask for His forgiveness and help."

"But I believe in all that—the cross, forgiveness."

"I'm sure it is true that you've heard it, but have you truly given your life to Christ?" There it was. The pivotal question.

Grace's pause lasted much too long. Finally, she whispered, "I can." She looked hopeful, uncertain.

Daniel's breath came out in a ragged sigh. This he had not anticipated. What could he do with such sweetly disarming honesty? He dropped his head and jammed his fingers into his hair. As much as he had wanted her willingness, already having guessed the answer would not be a straight "yes," his emotions were much too tied up in this.

"What?" she urged.

"Just as it's impossible for *me* to have enough faith to save *you*, this can't be something you do because of somebody else. It has to be because you truly want Christ in your life. And I wonder...you've been so hurt by your father...there's so much more you need to know about God."

"I can learn. Isn't it enough that I'm willing?"

"Yes, it's enough, but are you ready? Perhaps we should just take some time here. There's a lot to talk about, and maybe Amelia would be a good person to—"

But Grace stood up. Angelic face pale, slender body trembling, her breath came in tiny gasps. Daniel watched her like a man facing down a locomotive. He didn't want to hear what she was about to say, yet he was unable to stop it.

"I tell you everything about my past, even the most humiliating details. I open up my heart and hold nothing back. I confess to you that I am willing to give up everything in my current life so that I can be by your side. You tell me I'm a sinner, and even then, I am willing to pray this magic prayer that will make me acceptable to you. You lead me along...and then you slam the door in my face!"

Daniel stood. "Grace, please listen. I only thought—"

But she held up her hand, her eyes blazing. "No, you didn't think! And neither did I. I never dreamed the good, kind Rev. Monroe could be so judgmental, so cruel. Yes, my father has hurt me, but never so much as you. *He* never pretended to feel or be anything besides what he was."

The torrent of her words ripped a chasm in his heart as deep as the gorge a few hundred feet away. "The last thing I wanted to do was hurt you."

"Ah, famous last words. Couldn't you think of something more original than that?" Grace released a bitter laugh...so cold, so untouchable now. "Well, I suppose I deserve them. Maybe I've been the more foolish of the two of us because all this time, despite all we have said —you never once even told me you loved me."

"I love you."

He spoke the words softly, his arms hanging limp and helpless at his sides. He wanted to embrace her but couldn't. This encounter had underlined the truth, not changed it. For a moment, though, she stilled in response, and he dared to hope. Once more, he suggested, "Maybe if we just took some time, looked into the Bible about some of these things..."

Grace's expression congealed, and she took a step back. "At least in New York, they thought I was good enough." Then she turned and fled into the hotel.

~

*A*n oil lamp burned all night in Daniel's small Victorian cottage on the outskirts of Tallulah Falls. A new, attractive design, the house even boasted some of that gingerbread trim that was all the rage. A generous parishioner let it to him for a pittance. Not that Daniel's father couldn't have bought the place several times over, but Daniel liked to make his own way. It earned the respect of the townsfolk and gave him a sense of autonomy.

A man—even a bachelor—did have a mother, though. Inside, despite Daniel's sparse possession of furnishings, Evelyn Monroe had rendered unmistakable touches. She insisted on her younger son using certain pieces of family furniture, and she had graced the bare walls with a few choice paintings. That did make the quiet little place feel a bit more like home. He had even dreamed of one day bringing a wife here. Now, that possibility felt more remote than ever.

The first woman for whom he ever entertained more than a passing interest believed he disdained her. That he had led her on only to crush her with holier-than-thou, cold-hearted rejection. Maybe he had led her on. But if so, it had only been because he was a man, a human, who followed his heart. The sickening scene in the hotel garden was greatly his own fault.

Still, how could Grace misjudge him so? He hated to be misunderstood, but even more than that, he hated the hurt in her eyes. He hated that the way it looked right now, he could lose her forever.

Why had this happened? Why had he even met Grace if this was to be the end result? It was as if God had dangled a carrot in front of his face only to jerk it away.

He pushed that idea aside. He knew God better than that. His Father, as he had told Grace, was loving and kind, working even what seemed like disasters out for good and for His glory. Still, it seemed almost impossible to reckon that God's ultimate plan might include Daniel's words planting seeds in Grace's heart, rather than a continuing relationship. Why couldn't somebody else plant those seeds? Why couldn't he have come along after the harvest, able to reap a beautiful bride?

All night, he struggled with such questions, searching the Word of God, praying. What could he say to Grace? At last, he realized that, as usual, the wisest choice was to leave it in God's hands. And a still, small voice said to his heart, *Pray for her.*

Daniel surrendered. *All right, Lord. But in the morning, would it hurt to talk to Amelia? She's probably the only one Grace will listen to now.*

Before Daniel could determine an answer, as dawn streaked the horizon with faint color, he fell asleep.

～

he churning of his empty stomach woke him. Sprawled on the chair next to his kitchen table, draped over the open Bible, Daniel sat up. He rubbed his aching back and neck, blew out the lamp, and looked at the clock. Right at noon.

He didn't want to face people, but his empty cupboards attested to the fact that he hadn't visited the grocer in some time. Besides, he couldn't tolerate the thought of cooking in his present emotional state. How could his stomach could go on as though everything was normal when his heart had been crushed into a wad of wastepaper? He'd have to go to the café. Maybe he'd get lucky and find a table in the corner. But first, he'd have to change out of his white dress shirt and the fine black worsted wool trousers that matched his tailcoat.

Emerging a few minutes later in gray pants and vest and with his hair combed, Daniel squinted at the bright light. The bad thing about being the local minister was that he wasn't allowed to ever have a bad day. Everyone recognized him, waved to him, and expected his cheerful response and sincere inquiries into their health, both spiritual and physical.

He had to pass Wylie's Refreshments en route. He glimpsed Amelia inside in a sensible brown dress, handing a customer an ice cream sundae with a cherry on top. Should he stop now to talk to her? After lunch.

But as he passed the building, her voice called his name. He stopped and turned, noting her worried frown as she approached.

"You look awful," she announced with her usual tact.

"Thanks."

"Listen, I think you should know, I've...seen Grace."

"You have?" Daniel came to alertness.

Amelia wiped her hands on her ruffled apron. Or was it more wringing than wiping? "Yes. This morning. She told me a little about what had happened last night. I tried to explain things, help her see it from your viewpoint, but..."

"She was still too angry to listen?"

Amelia nodded, her mouth drawn into a flat line of sympathy and regret.

Daniel took his hat off, rubbed his hand over his face, then replaced the bowler. "Well, maybe in a few days."

Amelia's head shook. "Grace sent a message for me to come early this morning, and not just because she wanted to talk. She said goodbye. She left on the ten o'clock train."

His heart dropped to his toes. "*What*?"

"I'm sorry. I did all I could to dissuade her, but she'd made up her mind. I think her aunt and Mr. Greene were all too happy to oblige, despite the inconvenience of such a hasty departure. They didn't ask any questions. Anything to get her away from you. Mr. Greene even paid some outlandish price to buy tickets off a family. You know how many people are leaving town today."

Daniel took hold of Amelia's arms to stop her. "Why didn't you come get me?"

Amelia drew back, bristling at his rough behavior. "And how would that look?"

"Sorry," he muttered, his mind still churning. His gaze fell on the tracks gleaming in the distance, leading south. "Where did she go? Home?"

"Mr. Greene had offered a few weeks in Newport at his uncle's estate. Grace spoke of Monsieur LeMonte joining them there, resuming her daily practice. Getting ready for fall season."

"Mr. Greene, Mr. Greene!" The dandy would have her.

Daniel balled his fists. He kept looking at the tracks, as if he might grab a horse and ride after the train. No, that was stupid. Even if he caught up with her in Athens or Atlanta, he could say nothing new. Only God could make a difference now. If their love was meant to be, He could redeem Grace and bring her back. Daniel's shoulders slumped, and his breath exhaled in a deep sigh.

Amelia's eyes filled with a sheen of liquid pity. She placed a gentle hand on his arm. "I'm sorry, Daniel."

"It's all right, Amelia."

"What are you going to do now?"

That answer was, at last, easy. "Pray for her."

CHAPTER 12

November 18, 1886

My Dearest Amelia,

Well, I did it! I sang Aïda to a sold-out house six days ago. And in German, no less. At last, Monsieur LeMonte's coaching and string-pulling culminated in a glorious moment. Since then, fans deluge me with roses and chocolates, and the calling cards and invitations pile up in our tray. I can hardly appear in public without being accosted. But for all the flattery and sense of accomplishment, something is missing. It's your sweet, genuine face. Out of the many people I have met this year, you are the only one I would consider a friend.

I was surprised but happy to hear that Richard Callaway has been writing to you. I knew he really took a liking to you at Aunt Fannie's, I just never would have guessed he had the gumption to follow through. I know he's kind and you share some interests, but do you think he's exciting enough for you, Amelia, dear? Maybe if he visits again next summer as he hopes to do, you'll be able to tell.

Your letters have meant the world to me these past months, but I'm afraid they will no longer suffice. I'm enclosing train tickets for you and your parents and begging you, come spend Thanksgiving with us. We'll arrange a special box at the opera. We'll go to Tiffany's, Central Park, and The Statue of Liberty. You deserve to experience all the pleasures and sights of New York City. Please don't say no. Wire me when you are coming.

Your friend,

Grace Galveston

*G*race folded the gold-embossed page of stationery and dropped it, along with three tickets, into the envelope. She licked it and rang for the maid.

Ever since their return to New York, engagements filled every waking moment. When Grace's instructor released her from rehearsal, Blake escorted her to parties and dinners and took her for drives to view the brilliant autumn foliage of the surrounding countryside. New and fashionable friends called for tea, and Grace and Martha shopped for the recent cool-weather styles. Once Grace's father learned of her acceptance in the role of Aïda, his attentions renewed. Hampton belittled his disinterest in her summer escape by declaring he had known the North Georgia air would be her perfect cure.

Grace knew the air had worked no wonders. Before, her vulnerability exposed her to attacks of nerves, leaving her powerless to sing. Now, like a creature in a shell, her anger protected her. And, completely ignorant of his daughter's inner workings, Hampton attempted to bridge the gap with regular invitations to his Fifth Avenue home, an order for two Worth gowns, and a stunning set of emerald jewelry. He would hear no protests. No doubt, he wanted to make sure that his own involvement in her success did not go unaccredited.

But she could not allow Hampton's shallow overtures to arouse hope. She had opened her heart to viscous crushing too many times, the most recent the most devastating. Grace refused to think back to the sharpness of her heartache when she first left Tallulah Falls, the empty days without sight of Daniel's face and the long nights when she would lie awake and agonize over every word, every look, trying to find somewhere to lay the blame for his rejection. Yet, even now, as much as Grace attempted to fill her time to crowd out thoughts of him, she could not ignore the empty spot that still ached inside her.

Stable, caring, and fun, Amelia provided the answer. A perfect distraction. Grace could not wait to throw open her door to find her friend standing there.

When Maureen appeared in her gray frock, Grace

handed her the envelope and said, "Please post this at once."

~

*A*melia came, Tallulah's tourist off-season allowing her father to close up the soda shop. Grace basked in showing her friend all her favorite places and enjoying Amelia's awed responses. New York offered larger crowds, taller buildings, and more sophisticated amusements than the Wylies had ever experienced. They especially found the spectacle of the opera enthralling—the lavish scenes and costumes, the glinting jewels, the heart-stopping, soaring voices. And the elegance of Thanksgiving dinner with the Galvestons exceeded Tallulah's fine hotels.

But as much as Amelia praised her vacation of a lifetime, even letting Grace dress her up like a high-society debutante, she kept her head. She remained the same down-to-earth, unselfish girl from the mountains. And Grace loved her for it.

During their short time together, Grace maneuvered conversations and circumstances so that she and Amelia had no chance to stagnate on the topic of Daniel. But on the last day of Amelia's visit, something tugged at Grace's heart, imploring her to lower her guard.

As they nibbled cookies and drank milk in Grace's

bedroom, Maureen delivered a gift-wrapped box. The message accompanying it read, *A small adornment for my most precious jewel.*

Maureen, standing over her mistress, gasped when Grace sprung the latch. A diamond necklace glinted in the light.

Amelia rose to see what the fuss was about. "Who is it from?"

"Blake, of course." Grace held the beautiful gems up to her slender throat, admiring the effect. Then she shook her head, replaced the necklace, and snapped the lid shut. She held it out to Maureen. "Send it back."

"Miss?"

"He knows full well I can't accept such a gift without committing to marry him first. He's merely reminding me of the riches with which he'll shower me when I agree to become his bride."

Obedient, Maureen retreated, taking the box with her. But Amelia, who appeared bewildered by Grace's matter-of-fact tone, drew near. "*When?*" she repeated.

Grace turned on her dressing table stool, feeling almost apologetic, though for the life of her she didn't know why. "I told you in a letter how he proposed at Newport. Don't you remember? I made him promise to give me until Christmas for an answer."

"I thought then that pressing his advantage when you were hurt by another was...not right. I think now that plying you with expensive gifts is nothing short of bribery." Amelia put her hands on her hips. Clad in a cutwork lace nightgown and wrapper, she looked like an avenging angel.

Grace studied her for a minute, never having thought of it quite that way. Then she laughed. "Oh, Amelia. How I'm going to miss your plain speaking." She shrugged. "But why shouldn't I marry him? Despite what you may think, he *has* changed. He's become much more thoughtful and caring—and patient, agreeing to wait all this time."

"At least he's smart enough to act that way until he has you."

"Well, who would you have me marry?"

"No one, unless you love them."

Grace's gaze fell to the Persian carpet. Softly, she said, "The one I loved wouldn't have me."

Amelia bit her lip. At least she didn't repeat how difficult the parting had been for Daniel, rehashing of all the reasons he had not felt free to propose to Grace. A bunch of super-spiritual nonsense. She had registered her protest by refusing to attend church since returning to New York. But God didn't seem moved by her strike.

"Anyway," she went on, "even if your reverend came to me tomorrow on bent knee, I wouldn't have him. I wouldn't be able to trust him now any more than I do my father. No, I'm planning to accept Blake's proposal when he repeats it at Christmas. I care deeply for him, and the match makes perfect sense. Aunt Martha was right all along."

When Grace looked up, tears were filling Amelia's eyes—and running over! When the girl knelt in front of her and took her hands, Grace scooted back.

"Grace," she said, "*I'm* here on bent knee, and I hope you'll listen to me."

Grace tried to shake her off, but Amelia pressed on. "No. I've tried to say this before, but you didn't want to hear it. You've been so kind to me during my visit, but somehow you haven't been the same. Well, I'm going home tomorrow, so listen, anyway. My heart breaks over how hurt you've been, and how little love you've received. No wonder you're afraid of it! Your father has been wrong, crazy—and blind. Daniel—maybe he made mistakes, too, but he's just a man, a man who's in love with you and doesn't know what to do about it. Everyone messes up. Everyone will at some time disappoint you. As much as I want to always be your friend, someday I might too. There's only one Person who will *never* let you down."

"God is not a person."

"Of course, He is—in the God-man Jesus Christ, who promises that He will be a friend who sticks closer than a brother. Wait here."

Amelia got up, wiping her eyes, and scurried toward her bedroom. Grace sat, too stunned to disobey her. Moments later, Amelia returned, clutching a worn brown book. She laid it with reverence in Grace's lap. Grace turned questioning eyes upon her.

"My Bible. Actually, my first Bible. I used it a lot when I was younger." When Grace drew a breath to protest, Amelia held up her hand. "Don't worry, I have a new one now. This one will be of better use here with you. You'll notice I underlined a lot of passages and wrote in the margins. The Books of John and Romans are especially good."

She paused as if waiting for Grace to start thumbing through the pages on the spot. Grace didn't want to take the book, much less look through it, but she didn't want to hurt Amelia's feelings either. She looked so hopeful and vulnerable standing there wringing her hands.

"It will give you answers, Grace, it really will. It will show you God loves you and longs to heal your hurts and fill the hole in your heart."

How had Amelia known? Grace went to great lengths to keep anyone from suspecting that she felt so empty on the inside.

"Say something," Amelia urged.

"Thank you."

"You will keep it and look at it?"

Grace nodded.

"And write me any questions you might have?"

"I will."

Amelia smiled. Her shoulders relaxed. "Thank *you*, Grace, for making my dream of coming to New York come true. I've had such a wonderful time. You've been

—you *are*—like a sister to me. Even though we may be miles apart, you'll always be a dear friend." She bent down and threw her arms around Grace's mute form.

Overcome by surprise at Amelia's open-hearted speech and gesture, Grace sat on her dressing table stool, holding the Bible, long after her guest had gone to bed.

CHAPTER 13

*O*ver a week later, Grace stood at her bedroom window looking out over Gramercy Park. Even the cold gray drizzle and icy gusts of wind did not discourage the many citizens out on their holiday errands.

Earlier, Aunt Martha had insisted on the two of them going to view a flat on Fifth Avenue owned by a friend of Grace's father who had indicated he would make them a nice arrangement. Ecstatic, Martha had all but promised the friend's agent they were interested. On the way home, she shut out Grace's reservations.

If Grace protested outright, her aunt would be forced to comply. After all, the money belonged to Father, and by virtue of their relation, to Grace. But Grace did not like to dictate to her older relative. It seemed disrespectful of Aunt Martha's position and the years she had given as Grace's guardian. Aunt Martha

would at least have to listen to her concerns, though...
maybe later tonight when her aunt returned from her
round of visits.

This 1850s row house had been her only home. And
while the walnut and mahogany of the floors and built-
in appointments might not be as fashionable now as
lighter woods, Grace found them warm and comforting.
Knowing that her mother had lived here—if only for a
few short months—lodged at the heart of Grace's desire
to remain. Here, too, Maum Sally had trained Grace in
manners and morals—her presence, her stories, a
constant reminder of Louisa.

The area now housed many performing and visual
artists, so Grace still fit in just fine.

A knock sounded on her open door. She turned to
see Maureen standing there. "Your father is here to see
you, miss."

Her father...another obstacle to remaining in this
house.

"Please prepare a tea tray, Maureen."

Minutes later, Grace descended to the parlor. Her
father stood with his back to her, the card from a
bouquet of yellow roses cinched between two fingers.
He gave the flowers an idle sniff. Grace cleared her
throat, and he turned. Dark hair streaked with silver
framed angular features, while an elegant black
morning coat and tailored gray trousers enhanced a fit
physique and commanding manner. At the sight of his
daughter, he broke into a grin.

"It looks like a wake in here." He gestured to the veritable bower of arrangements sent by Grace's admirers.

Grace laughed and spread her hands in a helpless gesture. "They just keep coming."

"I'm afraid the scent is rather overpowering." Father stuck the card back amongst the roses.

"That's why they're all here and not in my room."

"Speaking of rooms, how did you like the flat?" His eyes lit with anticipation as he drew closer.

"Er...it was lovely. Quite fashionable."

Father grinned again. "No sense making the deliverymen drive all the way to Gramercy Park, eh? Besides, you'll be much more in your element on Fifth."

"Will I? You didn't seem to think so until this fall."

As soon as the words fell out, Grace bit her lip. This was not the approach she had meant to take. The Book of John in the Bible Amelia left with her portrayed a gentle Savior, one who used love to reach people. In Romans, she read exhortations to bless those who persecute you and not to be overcome by evil but overcome evil with good. Her recent biblical studies refreshed much that Maum Sally had taught her, including many Proverbs such as, *A soft answer turns away wrath, but a harsh word stirs up anger.*

The tea tray's arrival held at bay the darkening clouds of her father's expression. With shaking hands, Grace poured the hot liquid into two china teacups.

"Look," her father said, as if noticing her discomfiture, "I'm trying to make up for the wrongs of the past by doing right by you now."

"Then let me stay here."

"Here? Why?"

"*Why?* This is *home.*" Grace gestured around the room with her spoon. She plunked in a lump of sugar and stirred. "I like it here. I like the neighbors, I like the quiet, and most of all, I like the fact that I've lived here all my life."

"Don't you think it's time to move beyond your childhood?"

Grace stared at this man tied to her so closely by blood but really little more than a stranger, silently imploring him to realize how the lack of support during that very era produced such vulnerability now. When he merely stared back, she voiced another question. "And what if I fail? What if I don't continue on this path to stardom? How much will I belong on Fifth Avenue then?"

"You won't fail."

"But if I do—or if I'm unable to sing? Will you want to pay for that flat then?"

Father shifted in his seat, his tea untouched. "What you suggest is ridiculous, but if some emergency, some bad thing, were to happen, then of course, I would see you located wherever your needs were best served."

The master of the vague answer. Bitterness curdled in her stomach. "Mine? Or yours?"

"Look, what do you want from me, Grace? To move

into my house? That would hardly be appropriate, with your maiden aunt in tow."

"No! I want to stay here."

"Fine. No one's pushing you out, though I must admit, I've never seen anyone more resistive to advancement."

"Perhaps our priorities just aren't the same," Grace replied, then clamped her lips shut. Daniel had used almost those same words with her.

With a soft grumble, Hampton sat back in his wingchair and sipped his tea. "Just don't throw out the idea, Grace. Take some time and think it over. Consider the fact that the right address would not harm your prospects."

"Remember, I'm supposed to give Blake an answer this month. I hardly see why there's such a clamor to move considering that."

Father eyed her with shrewd assessment. "So you've decided to accept him?"

"I thought I had," Grace said softly, her mind drifting.

"*Thought*?"

"I have been planning to accept, but—oh, I don't want to talk about it..."

"Well, even if you do say yes, you'll have a long period of engagement with all the social activities that entails. Once an announcement confirms your future as a Greene, you'll be even more sought-after socially.

During that time, it makes sense for you to live close to me and your new circle of friends."

"With all that change before me, it seems all the more reason to stay secure in my own nest for a while."

"By the saints, you're a stubborn girl." A chuckle rumbled from his chest.

She laughed too. "Wonder where I got that from?"

Her father answered without hesitation. "Your mother."

Grace's eyebrows shot up. "You almost never talk about her. I've learned almost everything I know from Maum Sally and Aunt Martha. Why?"

"Some things are best left in the past."

"But don't you see, I need to know."

"*What* do you need to know?"

Grace bit her lip. While she longed to take advantage of this rare moment, this tenuous link between them, if she pressed too far, he might withdraw. "Everything...anything...but most especially, did you love her?"

Father gave no immediate confirmation, but a spark came into his eyes before he could retreat behind his mask of indifference. It made her imagine him younger, rasher, more vital. The way he had looked to her mother. The man he had been before abdicating his role in *her* life.

"We had a rocky relationship, your mother and I." He stared into space, into the past, as he spoke. "I saved her from a miserable fate but brought her into even more trouble. She never let me forget I was the enemy. Was it love or hate? I think, for me, if love is not being able to imagine life without that person...if losing them means trying every day to forget them...then I loved her."

Grace did not speak for a long time, digesting words she had waited so long to hear. They sank like water into her parched soul, yet deeper emotional thirst remained. One more question had surged with her every heartbeat for as long as she could remember.

"And...did you love me?" she whispered.

Father looked like Professor Leon probably did when the support line snapped. He blustered, shifted, moving his hat to his other knee. "Of course. I never blamed you for her loss. If I blamed anyone, it was myself."

"But then...why...?" Grace could not bring herself to finish the question. *Why did you move back home and leave us? Why didn't you take me with you? Why the infrequent visits, the distant manners, the lonely birthdays and Christmases? Why was I treated like your stepchild?*

Her heart might break with the longing. She didn't have to say all those things. He knew.

Father turned anguished eyes upon her. "Have you ever seen a picture of your mother?"

Grace shook her head. Any likenesses of Louisa had been destroyed in the fire.

"Every day, you grew more like her. Now you have but to look in the mirror."

As if he could stand no more, Father leapt to his feet and strode to the door. With a set face, he gathered up his great coat, scarf, and walking stick. But a strange new urging in her spirit told Grace she could not let him leave without saying one thing more. With tears in her eyes, she followed him to the foyer and stood in the parlor doorway.

"Father, I forgive you."

"What?" He turned to gape at her.

"I've been reading the Bible, and a dear friend told me that I had to let go of all the hurt inside. I can't keep being afraid of disappointing you. I can't keep being angry because you treat me like some illegitimate offspring when I am the daughter of your first love and wife. I want to be free. I don't want to be bitter. So"—she took a deep, gulping breath—"for everything...I forgive you."

With those words, Grace felt as she had the day Leon crossed the gorge, as if a great weight lifted off her chest and drifted up into the sky. The power in the words of Amelia's Bible had encouraged her, enabled her, to do this.

She might have hoped for tears or a hug, if not a belated apology. But Father looked...terrified. He jammed his hat on his head and left the house. So it had to be enough for now, this feeling of release.

Arms and legs trembling, Grace dragged herself up to her bedroom and closed the door. There on a little table lay the open Bible. She sank to the floor beside the table, lay her head on the seat of her rocking chair, and wept.

A long time later, she reached for the book. Wiping her eyes on her shawl, she thumbed again through the pages of Romans, where certain passages stood out, underlined a long time ago by her dear friend.

For all have sinned, and come short of the glory of God. But God commendeth His love toward us, in that, while we were yet sinners, Christ died for us. And for the wages of sin is death; but the gift of God is eternal life through Jesus Christ our Lord. And finally, if thou shalt confess with thy mouth the Lord Jesus, and shalt believe in thine heart that God hath raised him from the dead, thou shalt be saved.

"I surrender, Lord," Grace said out loud. "I give it all up, my hurts, my dreams, my fears. I don't want to live life like this anymore. Nothing else—no one else—has filled this terrible empty place inside my heart. Can You? If You can, I'll do whatever You want with the rest of my life."

She sank to the floor, spent, then surrounded and filled with the most indescribable sense of peace and perfect love.

CHAPTER 14

*D*aniel learned of the death of Saul Jones, a
favorite parishioner and former elder, on a
Saturday. Come Sunday morning, how would he deliver
the message he'd prepared earlier in the week, intended
to warm hearts for the coming celebration of Christ's
birth? It didn't seem fitting to move on so quickly. Jones
had been one of his strongest supporters from the time
Daniel's name came before Trinity Church for appoint-
ment. Even when crippled by advanced rheumatism,
Saul had attended faithfully, always ready with a word
of encouragement and a twinkle in his eye.

By Sunday afternoon, the body lay in the receiving
parlor, and the family gathered. Mrs. Jones met Daniel
at the door, arrayed in black. She would continue to
dress in the various stages of mourning—finally gradu-
ating to gray and lavender—for about two-and-a-half
years. Her house also echoed the traditional rites of

mourning, with a black ribbon on the doorknob, the mirrors covered with black crepe, and a vigil candle burning next to the coffin.

Daniel had been a frequent visitor in the Jones home, often having Sunday lunch and staying to play checkers or chess with Saul. So it didn't surprise him when Elizabeth Jones hugged his neck and burst into tears, despite the popular notion that a new widow should "hold up." He patted her back, a lump rising in his throat at the sight of the dear woman's grief.

At last, she pulled back and wiped her wrinkled cheeks with a damp handkerchief. "Ah, Rev. Monroe, 'tis a hard thing."

"I know it is, Mrs. Jones."

"Even though we'd known for some time his heart was weak—well, a woman's never prepared for her husband to die."

"He died in his sleep?"

She nodded. "And looks more peaceable now than I've seen him in years, what with the rheumatism."

Daniel went with her into the receiving parlor, where he sat for some time with the family, praying with them and comforting them with Scripture. There were quiet tears but no agonized sobbing.

"Thank you for coming by, Rev. Monroe," Mrs. Jones said when he rose to take his leave. "Saul is with the Lord now. And that's the biggest comfort of all."

Donning his hat and overcoat, Daniel left the house. A peaceful, early snow fell, making for a beautiful scene as he walked back toward town. He pulled his lapels up around his neck.

The biggest challenge ahead of Elizabeth did not entail settling any question of Saul's eternal destiny, but of releasing her best friend to the Lord and finding the strength to face each day without him. They had enjoyed a long and fruitful life together. That's what Daniel had always hoped for—a soul mate, a partner.

When he looked ahead to officiating over Saul's funeral on the morrow, followed by a string of advent sermons and celebrations, Daniel sighed. He lacked any vestige of holiday cheer. For Christmas, his brother and sister-in-law would visit from Darien, making three happy couples at Crown Pointe, plus Daniel. He didn't want to face any of it.

The Lord seemed to whisper in his ear. *When you are weak, I am strong.*

Hadn't he lived all autumn on the promise in Jeremiah that God wanted not to harm him, but to give him a future and a hope? *I know You are enough. But I can't help it. I want human companionship too.*

Loneliness almost turned his steps toward the town. There would be a cozy little gathering around the woodstove at Wylie's, talking, laughing, and drinking hot chocolate. The one person who understood how he felt would be there.

His mother had gently urged him to start looking for romance closer to home. While she had liked Grace and had discerned the spark between Grace and her son, she couldn't bear to witness Daniel's continuing sadness.

If he went to Wylie's now and asked Amelia to take a walk with him in the snow, she would know. She would realize that he was attempting to move toward something more than friendship. Maybe the passion he didn't feel now would come with time.

But instead, Daniel found himself cutting off the main road on the path that led to Lover's Leap. As he trudged through the woods, the dead leaves under his feet receiving their slow baptism of silent white flakes, he thought about the talk he'd had with Amelia after she'd returned from New York. He had been so encouraged to learn that Grace accepted Amelia's Bible. God could work wonders once His Word got into a person's hands.

But then Amelia had gone on, with her gentle honesty, to describe Grace's glittering lifestyle, Blake's ardent courtship, and how Grace intended to marry the young lawyer.

"Keep praying," Amelia had told him, "but I don't want to raise any false hopes. Even if she finds the Lord, she might never leave New York."

And she might marry Blake. For even though Daniel was willing to move north, that would not matter if Blake had already managed to capture her heart. After all, Blake had been there all this time to spread the generous salve of his sympathetic attention on her wounds.

When he reached the overlook, Daniel sat on a fallen log and removed a photograph from his vest pocket. Grace, clinging to his arm as they stood on this very spot, smiled at him in sepia tones. He was glad she had been laughing when Hunnicutt took the picture, instead of striking a traditionally somber pose. It made her so much more lifelike. He could almost see the roses in her cheeks and smell the sweet fragrance of her hair.

For the hundredth time, Daniel asked God to remove his longing for this woman if their love was not meant to be.

Something rustled behind him. Probably a squirrel. Daniel continued with his prayers. But the next moment, when a voice spoke, he jumped up and turned.

"The locals say that at this very spot, an Indian maiden leaped off the precipice after the man she loved, unwilling to live without him."

Given the amazing picture that met his eyes, Daniel must be hallucinating. Before him stood the very object of his thoughts. A hooded cloak of white fur that fell below her knees and made her seem a product of the snowy surroundings framed Grace's red-gold hair and brown eyes. A figment of his imagination. He jammed the photo back into his vest and stood staring at her, mouth slightly open.

"I understand how she felt," Grace added softly.

"What—how are you here?"

"Train." She raised one brow in a teasing gesture. "I wired Amelia that I was coming. She told me where you were when I got here, so I walked out to meet you. I saw you turn off the road."

His heart started to beat again. He took a step forward. Suddenly, the meaning of her words about the Indian maiden dawned on him, and the blood went rushing through his veins. "I guess what I meant to ask was *why* did you come?" He managed to keep his voice calm. "It's hardly tourist season."

She smiled, and the tranquility radiating from her struck him. "I had to tell you in person that I made peace with my Father."

"You did? Why, that's wonderful, Grace! Did he come with you?"

Again, the enigmatic smile that left him bemused. "I guess you could say so." Then she laughed and put a gloved hand to her heart. "I didn't mean that father... although I did forgive him for everything in the past. I meant *our* Father."

"Oh, Grace! Thank God!" Joy overpowered Daniel's confusion, and he leapt forward, grabbing her lithe figure in a bear hug.

She laughed, her breath puffs of white in the frosty air. "You were right." She pulled back a bit to look at him. "I needed to deal with a lot before I was ready to become *any* man's wife. Regardless of what has happened, or will happen, I wanted to tell you that in person." A moment of hesitation crossed her features.

Daniel sobered. Grace could have simply written to him about finding peace with God. Then there was her emphasis on that one tiny word, *any*. Daniel tamped down the hope spiraling inside him. He couldn't stand it if she had come all this way only for closure. He drew a breath. "Amelia told me Blake proposed, and that you were to give him an answer by Christmas."

Grace nodded. "All this fall, I planned to accept. His attentions were so soothing after my hurt." When he tried to speak, she held up her hand. "I'm ready to own my part in what happened. Whatever you did or didn't do, it doesn't matter now, because I understand the position you were in. At least...I hope I do..." She paused, gazing up at him through thick lashes with a hopeful, almost coy, expression.

"Thank you, Grace, but...about Blake?" Daniel couldn't endure the suspense a moment longer.

"I realized I could not marry a man I didn't love."

Daniel's breath exhaled in a whoosh.

"I told him that just before I left to come here. He was disappointed, of course, but not crushed—for I don't believe he truly loved me either."

Trying to take this in, Daniel hung his head and closed his eyes, still holding her arms in a light grasp. After all the time he spent waiting and hoping, the scene felt surreal.

Grace continued, composed, as if oblivious to the effect of her words. "Besides, now that I've had a taste of stardom, I'm not sure that being a celebrity suits me. It has its perks, but I've always suspected I was made for a more modest lifestyle. It would hardly be fair to Blake to ask him to leave the city he loves, where he works, when I might relocate."

"Relocate?" Had she had a better offer from another opera company?

"Yes, a dear friend just told me there could be an opening for a soprano in the Christmas cantata at Tallulah's Trinity Episcopal Church. When I got on the train, I knew I was taking a chance, coming here, but I felt this urging inside that I couldn't ignore. So...what do you think? About that opening?"

"I think," Daniel said slowly, "I hope...that God might just be giving a lonely minister his heart's desire." His pulse raced. Would the future he longed for dissipate like the mist of his breath?

"If what you say is true, a girl would need a proper invitation to stay." Grace looked into his eyes. "Like redheads are apt to do, I rushed ahead once before."

"You're sure? You would be giving up the supreme accomplishment of which any singer could dream. We could consider me joining you—"

She put a finger over his lips. "Thank you, but I've already spoken my heart on this matter, more than once." A tiny smile belied the scolding words.

Daniel captured her hand, tugged off the glove, and kissed her skin. He took a deep, steadying breath. "In that case, Miss Grace Galveston, will you do me the great honor of becoming my bride?"

"I love you, Daniel Monroe, and I will."

Daniel laughed. His heart might burst from the fullness of joy, the wonder at God's sense of timing and irony. Daniel could almost imagine Him laughing too.

"I love you, Grace. But I can hardly believe this isn't a dream. There's not been a day since you left that I haven't thought of you."

"Nor I of you."

"I guess that says it all."

"Then you can finally kiss me."

Daniel bent his head and ever so slightly brushed his lips across hers, afraid that at his touch, she might disintegrate like the falling snow. But her lips felt soft and incredibly warm. She was real. This was real. He started to draw back to gaze at her just to make sure, but Grace caught his head and pressed her mouth to his, providing all the confirmation he needed. His embrace lifted her feet off the ground, and he kissed her as he'd longed to for the past six months.

When they finally parted, Grace gasped. "Now *that* was worth the fuss I created when I left New York!"

"You came alone?"

She shrugged. "I made Maureen accompany me."

"Your aunt was livid," Daniel said with certainty.

"We'll pray for her, and she'll come around." She smirked.

"And the opera?"

"They can call up that Herbert-Forster woman whose husband plays in the orchestra."

Daniel smiled and took Grace's hand. "We once talked about how beautiful the gorge was covered in snow. Come, my love. Let me show you." He pulled her gently to the edge of the precipice and wrapped his arms around her.

There they stood for a long time, looking out over Lover's Leap together.

EPILOGUE

*nd that was the beginning of my great-great-grandparents' life together.

The way I hear it told, Aunt Martha wasn't too crushed at the prospect of moving to Tallulah Falls herself, once Professor Schmidt made bold to tell her of his feelings. As she settled into life in North Georgia, the Southland settled like balm around her soul. Its soothing tones and balmy days melted away that shell she wore. And after sitting under enough of Daniel Monroe's sermons, she, too, made peace with her past and with her Lord.

When Hampton Galveston realized his daughter truly loved this Appalachian minister and was set to live her life with him, he, too, gave his blessing. He even agreed to come to the little church to give her away in a July wedding. That visit, and a growing bond with his daughter, convinced him that the mountain resort would be a perfect new vacation spot for his family.

In the years that followed, folks brought their children from miles around to be tutored by the great operatic singer Grace Galveston Monroe. She became a legend in these parts. Many a career was launched from the Monroes' parlor. Four children and twenty-two years later, the Rev. Mrs. Monroe became a member of the faculty at the new Tallulah Falls School, oft called "The Light in the Mountains."

Yes, it's quiet here now. The grand era of tourism is over. The river's dammed up. Several times a year, they have what they call "aesthetic releases." I go and watch the kayakers ensconced in their bright little boats plunging over the waterfalls, temporarily restored to their former power and glory. Only once since the summer of 1886 has Tallulah Falls seen crowds like they did then—in 1970, when another famous aerialist, Karl Wallenda, crossed the gorge on a high wire.

Yet I can imagine how it used to be. Sometimes as I sit looking out over the gorge, I consider with pride the people like my ancestors who called this land home. The legacy of music and faith Grandma Grace left to both her pupils and her descendants still lives on today. A bit of it is inside my heart.

Did you enjoy this book? We hope so!
**Would you take a quick minute to leave a review
where you purchased the book?**
It doesn't have to be long. Just a sentence or two telling
what you liked about the story!

Receive a FREE ebook and get updates when new Wild
Heart books release: https://wildheartbooks.org/
newsletter

ACKNOWLEDGMENTS

This novella was originally released as *Redeeming Grace* by Publish America in 2006. Many books later, I'm pleased to bring it to a broader public as part of the Romance at the Gilded Age Resorts Series with Wild Heart Books. A big thank you to Misty Beller and the staff for making this possible.

While the central characters in *A Summer at the Niagara of the South* have been fictional, I hope their story captured your imagination and provided a realistic glimpse of Tallulah Falls c. 1886. I created Trinity Episcopal for this love story, but the St. James Mission (Episcopal) began near the falls in the early 1880s. According to *Images of America: Tallulah Falls*, a church building was constructed c. 1890. The website of beautiful Grace-Calvary Episcopal in Clarkesville provides the fascinating history of Grace Church as well as missions on the area circuit.

Some of the individuals mentioned in the story, like the Moss family, "Aunt Fannie" Smith, and Professor Leon, truly did shape Tallulah Falls in the late 1800s. I would like to thank Brian A. Boyd, communications director at Tallulah Falls School, and author of my most-used resource, *Secrets of Tallulah*, for his generous help in clarifying details about Victorian Tallulah. Special thanks also are due to Mr. John Moss for providing information on his ancestors.

Many visitors enjoy the beauty of Tallulah Gorge State Park every year. The Jane Hurt Yarn Interpretive Center provides wonderful information on the history, flora and fauna, and wildlife of the area. Aesthetic water releases from the dam are held each spring and fall.

Other sources consulted include *Habersham County, Georgia: A Pictorial History* by Jo and Stephen Whited; *Georgia Waters: Tallulah Falls, Madison Springs, Scull Shoals and the Okefenokee Swamp* by E. Merton Coulter, 1965; *The Appalachian Forest* by Chris Bolgiano, Stack-Pole Books, 1998; *Where There Are Mountains: An Environmental History of the Southern Appalachians* by Donald Edward Davis, The University of Georgia Press, 2000; *Georgia Magazine* August 1971 article "Aunt Fannie Smith: The Famous Hostess of Sinking Mountain" by Michael Motes; Athens, Georgia, *Daily News*, Sunday, May 15, 1966 article "Family Puzzlers" by Mary Bondurant Warren; *Kobbé's Complete Opera Book ed. & rev. by The Earl of Harewood, G. P. Putnam's Sons, NY, 1954; and numerous web sites on The Metropolitan Opera's history, Victorian-era New York City society, fashion, music, dance, the 131st New York Volunteer Infantry, historic Darien, Georgia, and historic Habersham County, Georgia.*

If you enjoyed this story, please consider leaving an online review. You can read about my other novels at https://www.deniseweimerbooks.com, and I'd also love to connect on social media.

Monthly e-mail list: http://eepurl.com/dFfSfn

https://www.facebook.com/denise.weimer1

https://twitter.com/denise_weimer

https://www.bookbub.com/profile/denise-weimer

ABOUT THE AUTHOR

North Georgia native Denise Weimer has authored over a dozen traditionally published novels and a number of novellas—historical and contemporary romance, romantic suspense, and time slip. As a freelance editor and Acquisitions & Editorial Liaison for Wild Heart Books, she's helped other authors reach their publishing dreams. A wife and mother of two daughters, Denise always pauses for coffee, chocolate, and old houses.

GET ALL THE BOOKS IN THE
ROMANCE AT THE GILDED AGE
RESORTS SERIES

A Winter at the White Queen
By Denise Weimer

A Summer at Sagamore
By Lisa M. Prysock

A Season at the Grand
By Sherri Wilson Johnson

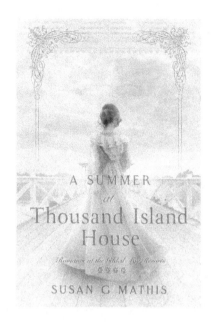

A Summer at Thousand Island House
By Susan G. Mathis

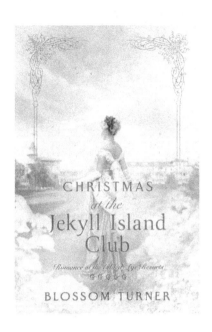

Christmas at the Jekyll Island Club
By Blossom Turner

A Summer on Bellevue Avenue
By Lorri Dudley

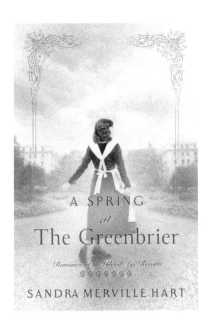

A Spring at The Greenbrier
By Sandra Merville Hart

WANT MORE?

If you love historical romance, check out the other Wild Heart books!

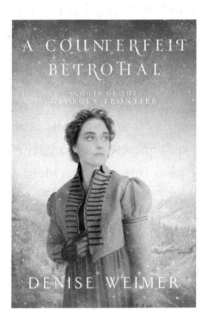

A Counterfeit Betrothal by Denise Weimer

A frontier scout, a healing widow, and a desperate fight for peace.

At the farthest Georgia outpost this side of hostile Creek Territory in 1813, Jared Lockridge serves his country as a scout to redeem his father's botched heritage. If he can help secure peace against Indians allied to the British, he can bring his betrothed to the home he's building and open his cabinetry shop. Then he comes across a burning cabin and a traumatized woman just widowed by a fatal shot.

Freed from a cruel marriage, Esther Andrews agrees to winter at the Lockridge homestead to help Jared's pregnant sister-in-law. Lame in one foot, Esther has always known she is secondhand goods, but the gentle carpenter-turned-scout draws her heart with as much skill as he creates furniture from wood. His family's love offers hope even as violence erupts along the frontier—and Jared's investigation into local incidents brings danger to their doorstep. Yet how could Esther ever hope a loyal man like Jared would choose her over a fine lady?

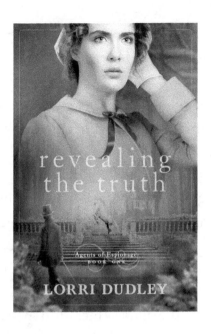

Revealing the Truth by Lorri Dudley

His suspect holds a secret, but can he uncover the truth before she steals his heart?

When Katherine Jenkins is rescued from the side of the road, half-frozen and left for dead, her only option is to stay silent about her identity or risk being shipped back to her ruthless guardian, who will kill to get his hands on her inheritance and the famous Jenkins Lipizzaner horses. But even under the pretense of amnesia, she cannot shake the memory of her sister and Katherine's need to reach her before their guardian, or his marauding bandits, finish her off. Will she be safe in the earl's manor, or will the assailant climbing through her window be the death of her?

British spy, Stephen Hartington's assignment to uncover an underground horse-thieving ring brings him home to his family's manor, and the last thing he expected was to be struck with a candlestick upon climbing through the guest chamber window. The manor's feisty and intriguing new house guest throws Stephen's best-laid plans into turmoil and raises questions about the timing of her appearance, the convenience of her memory loss, and her impeccable riding skills. Could he be housing the horse thief he'd been ordered to capture—or worse, falling in love with her?

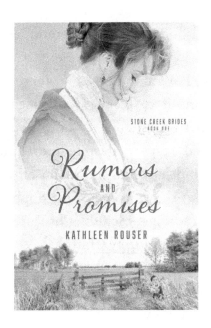

Rumors and Promises by Kathleen Rouser

She's an heiress hiding a tumultuous past. He's a reverend desperate to atone for his failures.

Abandoned by her family, Sophie Biddle has been on the run with a child in tow. At last, she's found a safe life in Stone Creek, Michigan, teaching piano. But when a kind, yet meddling and handsome, minister walks into her life seeking to help, Sophie is caught off guard and wary. When her secrets threaten to be exposed, will she be able to trust the reverend, and more importantly, God?

After failing his former flock, Reverend Ian McCormick is determined to start anew in Stone Creek, and he's been working harder than ever to forget his mistakes and prove himself to his new congregation—and to God. But when he meets a young woman seeking acceptance and respect, despite the rumors swirling about her sordid past, Ian finds himself pulled in two directions. If he shows concern for Sophie's plight, he could risk everything—including his position as pastor of Stone Creek Community Church.

Will the scandals of their pasts bind them together or drive them apart forever?

Printed in the USA
CPSIA information can be obtained
at www.ICGtesting.com
JSHW011359310524
63792JS00007B/32